根据教育部《大学英语课程教学要求》编写

总 主 编	李庆明
副总主编	杨真洪　尹丕安　黄雯琴
主 编	宋改荣
副 主 编	叶西平　郑爱香　高红莉
编 者	李咏梅　戴彬彬　崔小清
	王巧宁　杨玉霞

普通高等院校大学英语"十一五"重点规划教材

COLLEGE ENGLISH READING COURSE

Student's Book

大学英语阅读教程 III

西北工业大学出版社

【内容简介】 《大学英语阅读教程(Ⅰ～Ⅳ)》是高等学校非英语专业的阅读教材,旨在帮助大学生尽快适应大学英语阅读的模式及难度,为最终突破大学英语四、六级阅读难关打下坚实的基础。各分册均有 12 个单元,每单元均包含 4 篇文章:1 篇快速阅读、1 篇选词填空仔细阅读、2 篇多项选择仔细阅读,并配有词汇、注释及其练习。

　　本教程可作为高等学校英语阅读教材,尤其适合在校大学生备考大学英语四、六级使用,同时对自学者提高英语阅读能力也大有裨益。

图书在版编目(CIP)数据

大学英语阅读教程/李庆明主编 . —西安:西北工业大学出版社,2008.7
ISBN 978 - 5612 - 2416 - 8

Ⅰ. 大…　Ⅱ. 李…　Ⅲ. 英语—阅读教学—高等学校—教材　Ⅳ. H319.4

中国版本图书馆 CIP 数据核字(2008)第 096978 号

出版发行:西北工业大学出版社
通信地址:西安市友谊西路 127 号　邮编:710072
电　　话:(029)88493844　88491757
网　　址:www.nwpup.com
印 刷 者:陕西宝石兰印务有限责任公司
开　　本:787 mm×1 092 mm　　1/16
印　　张:39.125
字　　数:908 千字
版　　次:2008 年 7 月第 1 版　2008 年 7 月第 1 次印刷
定　　价:96.00 元(本册 24.00 元,附同步学习光盘 1 张)

《大学英语自学教程》编委会

前言

　　为了适应我国高等教育新的发展形势,深化教学改革,提高教学质量,满足新时期国家对人才培养的需求,教育部 2005 年 9 月公布了大学英语四、六级考试题型改革的新题型,同时,改革分数的报告形式,由原来的 100 分制改为 710 分制。其主要目的是使得该项考试更能准确地考查我国在校大学生的英语综合应用能力。

　　这次大学英语四、六级考试题型改革无论是从深度还是广度上都是史无前例的。然而,比较新旧题型中阅读理解所占的比重,我们不难发现其变化甚微,只是在考查方式上变得多样化了。从单纯的考查仔细阅读能力变为现在综合考查阅读能力,既考查仔细阅读能力,也考查快速阅读能力,同时还考查大学生通过上下文推测词义和内容的能力。现代外语教育理论认为,阅读能力是增强英语综合应用能力的基础,是提高学生外语文化素质的桥梁。阅读能力的提高,必定会深层次地提高学习者的跨文化交际能力和文化素质。

　　基于此,为了便于大学生尽快适应大学英语四、六级考试新题型,充分提高他们的阅读理解能力和综合应用能力,我们悉心研究了《大学英语课程教学要求(试行)》和《全国大学英语四、六级考试改革方案(试行)》,组织西安理工大学的资深教师根据其精神和要求精心编写了本系列大学英语阅读教程。本系列教程的大部分内容经过几年的使用,证明了对提高学习者的阅读应试能力、综合应用能力有很大作用。全套书共四册,各册严格按照大学英语难度分级标准设计,每册都包含快速阅读和仔细阅读所涉及的三类题型的练习,是检验学习者阅读能力梯级提高的良师益友。整套系列设计符合外语学习循序渐进的学习原则。

　　全套书的每册均分为 12 个单元,每单元均包括 4 篇阅读文章。第一篇为快速阅读,后附练习题,Words & Expressions,Notes 以及 Key to the Exercises。第二篇为选词填空,后附练习题,Words & Expressions,

Notes 以及 Key to the Exercises。第三、四篇为仔细阅读，后附练习题，Words & Expressions，Notes 以及 Key to the Exercises。

本册为第三册，依照大学英语四级阅读的难度、长度、题材、体裁等要求编写。内容均选自地道的英美报刊文摘，题材涉及面广，内容丰富多彩，题目设计合理规范，是广大大学生提高阅读能力，攻破四级考试大关的得力助手，也是一般英语爱好者扩大知识面，了解英美文化的一个桥梁。

本系列教程每册都配有多媒体光盘 1 张，作为教材内容的延伸和定时阅读训练的辅助手段。

本系列教程在编写过程中得到了西北工业大学出版社的大力支持，在此对出版社领导和编辑表示衷心的感谢！

由于作者水平等原因，本系列教程中仍可能存在不妥之处，真诚欢迎各位专家和读者提出建议，批评指正，我们将在重印和改版时加以改进。

编　者

目录

Unit 1

Passage 1

Directions

There are 10 questions after the passage. Go over the passage quickly and answer the questions in the given time.

For questions 1 – 7, mark

Y(for YES)   if the statmenet agrees with the information given in the passage;

N(for NO)   if the statement contradicts the information given in the passage;

NG(for NOT GIVEN) if the information is not given in the passage.

For questions 8 – 10, complete the sentences with the information given in the passage.

How to Talk to Your Kids

Every family is different, with different personalities, customs, and ways of thinking, talking, and connecting to one another. There is no one "right" kind of family. But whether parents are strict or lenient, boisterous or calm, home has to be a place of love, encouragement, and acceptance of their feelings and individuality for kids to feel emotionally safe and secure. It also has to be a source of don'ts and limits.

Most of us want such an atmosphere to prevail in our homes, but with today's stress this often seems harder and harder to achieve. From time to time it helps to take stock and think about the changes we could make to improve our home's emotional climate. Here are a few that will.

Watch what you say

How we talk to our children every day is part of the emotional atmosphere we weave.

Besides giving them opportunities to be open about how they feel, we have to watch what we say and how we say it.

We often forget how much kids take parental criticisms to heart and how much these affect their feelings about themselves. Psychologist Martin Seligman found that when parents consistently blame kids in exaggerated ways, children feel overly guilty and ashamed and withdraw emotionally. Look at the difference between "Roger, this room is always a pigsty! You are such a slob (懒汉)!" and "Roger, your room is a mess today! Before you go out to play, it has to be picked up."

One way tells Roger he can never do anything right. The other tells him exactly what to do to fix things so he can be back in his mom's good graces and doesn't suggest he has a permanent character flaw. For criticism to be constructive for children, we have to cite causes that are specific and temporary.

Another constructive way to criticize children is to remind them of the impact their actions have on us. This promotes empathy rather than resentment.

Provide order and stability

A predictable daily framework, clear and consistent rules, and an organized house make kids and parents more relaxed and comfortable, and that means everyone has emotional equilibrium. When conflicts, tensions, or crises occur, the routine is a reassuring and familiar support, a reliable strand of our lives that won't change.

Think about your mornings. Do your kids go off to school feeling calm and confident? Or are they upset and grumpy (脾气坏的)?

What about evenings and bedtime? Do you have angry fights over homework or how much TV children can watch? A calm bedtime routine is one good antidote for the dark fears that surface when kids are alone in bed with the lights turned off.

Yet a routine that's too inflexible doesn't make room for kids' individual temperaments, preferences, and quirks (怪癖).

Hold family meetings

Time together is at such a premium in most households that many families, like the Martins, hold regular family meetings so everyone can air and resolve the week's grievances as well as share the good things that happened.

When the Martins gather on Friday night, they also take the opportunity to anticipate what's scheduled for the week ahead. That way they eliminate those last-minute anxieties over whether someone has soccer shoes for the first practice, the books for a report, or a ride to a music lesson.

Encourage loving feelings

Everyday life is full of opportunities to establish loving connections with our kids.

Researchers have found that parents who spend time playing, joking with, and sharing their own thoughts and feelings with their kids have children who are more friendly, generous, and loving.

After all, giving love fosters love, and what convinces our kids that we love them more than our willingness to spend time with them? Many parents say that often they feel most in tune emotionally with their kids when they just hang out together—sprawling on the bed to watch TV, walking down the block together to mail a letter, talking on long car rides when kids know they have a parent's complete attention. At these times the hurt feelings and the secret fears are finally mentioned.

Part of encouraging loving feelings is insisting that kids treat others, including siblings, with kindness, respect, and fairness—at least some of the time. In one family, kids write on a chart in the kitchen at the end of each day the name of someone who did something nice for them.

Create rituals

Setting aside special time of the day or week to come together as a family gives children a sense of continuity—that certain feelings stay the same even as the kids change and grow. For many families, like my friend Frances', that means regularly observing religious rituals. To her family, Sunday morning means going to Mass and having hot chocolate afterwards at the town café. Others create their own rituals to anchor the week. Michael's family celebrates with a regular scrabble (一种拼字游戏) and pizza party every Friday night; Dawn's goes to the movies. Holiday rituals give children points in the year to look forward to.

Handle challenges with compassion

Home life today is not always stable and secure. Even the best marriages have fights, economic woes, emotional ups-and-downs. Parents divorce, stepfamilies form, and these changes challenge the most compassionate parents. But troubles are part of the human condition. Loving families don't ignore them—they try to create a strong emotional climate despite them.

In handling parental conflicts, for example, we can let kids know when everything has been resolved, as Denise and Peter did after a loud dispute in the kitchen during which voices were raised and tears flowed. After making up, they explained to their kids, "Sometimes we disagree and lose our tempers, too. But now we've worked it out. We're sorry that you overheard our fight."

Schedule parent-only time

Parents are the ones who create a home's atmosphere. When we're upset about how much money we owe, worried about downsizing at the company where we work, or angry at a spouse, that Changes the emotional atmosphere in ways kids find threatening. As one friend said plaintively, "Parents need special time, too." Taking a long walk together to talk without our kids may go a long way to soothe worries and regular "parent-only" dates help us re-experience the love that brought us together in the first place.

Approximate Length: 1,068 words
Suggested reading time: 8 minutes
How fast do you read? _____

Comprehension Exercises

Complete the following exercises without referring back to the passage you have read.

1. Families tend to have similar patterns.
2. Children usually don't care about how and what their parents say to them.
3. Parents should have consistent requirements for their children.
4. Children are not allowed to talk at family meetings.
5. Parents' staying with children can promote love between parents and children.
6. Best marriages never have troubles such as fights, emotional ups-and-downs.
7. It is good to take children abroad for travel.
8. Home is a place where children can feel emotionally _____.
9. Setting aside special time of the day or week to come together as a family gives children _____.
10. In handling parental conflicts, parents had better tell their children that _____.

Words & Expressions

1. **lenient** *adj.* 宽大的;仁慈的;慈悲为怀的
2. **prevail** *vi.* 流行,盛行
   e.g. This custom still prevails in some parts of the country. 这一风俗仍在该国的某些地区盛行。
3. **equilibrium** *n.* 平衡,平静,均衡,保持平衡的能力;沉着,安静
4. **consistently** *adv.* 一贯地;始终如一地
5. **temperament** *adj.* 气质;性情;秉性
   e.g. a sunny temperament 开朗的性格
6. **grievance** *n.* 不平;委屈;不满
7. **anticipate** *vt.* 预期;预料
   e.g. It is anticipated that next year interest rates will fall. 人们预计明年的利率会下调。
8. **premium** *n.* 额外费用,奖金,奖赏;保险费

at a premium 奇缺

e. g. premium payment for weekend work 周末工作津贴

Insurance premiums are set to rise again. 保险费很有可能再次上涨。

9. **compassion** *n.* 怜悯；同情

e. g. compassion for the poor and the sick 对穷人和病人的同情

10. **sprawl** *vi.* （懒洋洋地）伸开手脚坐/躺着

11. **soothe** *vi.* 抚慰，安慰；使平息

e. g. Rocking often soothes a crying baby. 轻摇常常可以让一个哭泣的婴儿安静下来。

Notes

1. It also has to be a source of don'ts and limits. 家庭也必须是约束和限制孩子的地方。

2. Psychologist Martin Seligman found that when parents consistently blame kids in exaggerated ways, children feel overly guilty and ashamed and withdraw emotionally. 心理学家 Martin Seligman 发现，当父母总是言过其实地责备孩子时，孩子就会感到过度内疚和羞愧，从而在情感上与父母不合。

3. For criticism to be constructive for children, we have to cite causes that are specific and temporary. 要使批评对孩子有帮助，我们必须给孩子说出当时挨批的具体理由。

4. Even the best marriages have fights, economic woes, emotional ups-and-downs. 再美满的婚姻也免不了有争吵、经济压力及情感上的波动。

5. When we're upset about how much money we owe, worried about downsizing at the company where we work, or angry at a spouse, that changes the emotional atmosphere in ways kids find threatening. 我们会为家底而心烦，担心所在公司裁员，或者对配偶不满，孩子对这样的家庭气氛会感到害怕。

Key to the Exercises

1. N   2. N   3. Y   4. N   5. Y   6. N   7. NG   8. safe and secure

9. a sense of continuity   10. everything has been solved

Passage 2

> ### Directions
>
> *In this section, there is a passage with 10 blanks. You are required to select one word for each blank from a list of choices given in a word bank following the passage. Read the passage through carefully before making your choices. Each choice in the bank is identified by a letter. Please choose the corresponding letter*

for each item. You may not use any of the words in the bank more than once.

Tips on Safe Driving

The number one passenger safety precaution is to make sure everyone is __1__ buckled up. Before leaving on vacation, have your vehicle checked to make sure it's safe. Repair or replace worn parts to avoid the worry and time-consuming costly repairs that could __2__ your trip. Check all tires, for condition and tire pressure including the __3__ tire. Replace your windshield wiper blades if they are worn or __4__. Make sure all lights work, including signal lights. Carry a flashlight, flares and first-aid __5__, where they can be reached easily in case of an __6__. Sunglasses, road maps, a notebook, and a pencil or pen will all come in handy.

When you buy gas, always spend a few minutes on simple __7__. Check oil and other fluids. Clean the windshield and other glass __8__ including headlights and taillights. This will help increase your mileage and reduce your service costs.

Fatigue is a form of impairment, so don't give in to that temptation to push on. If you start early, stop early. If you feel __9__, have a good sleep before you take the wheel. It might be better to delay your trip until the morning. Rest stops are important. A break keeps the driver __10__ by promoting blood circulation, makes the trip more pleasant for passengers and lets the vehicle cool down.

Approximate Length：226 words

A. spoil   B. survival   C. spare
D. cracked   E. persistence   F. kit
G. emergency   H. enraged   I. maintenance
J. engagement   K. surfaces   L. offended
M. fatigued   N. alert   O. properly

1. _____   2. _____   3. _____   4. _____   5. _____
6. _____   7. _____   8. _____   9. _____   10. _____

Words & Expressions

1. **precaution** *n.* 预防措施

   e.g. Fire precautions were neglected. 防火措施被忽略了。

2. **windshield** *n.* 挡风玻璃

3. **wiper blades** 刮水片

4. **come in handy** 迟早会有用

e. g. Take the knife with you on your trip. It may come in handy. 上路时把这把小刀带在身边,说不定用得上。

5. **mileage** *n.* （一般用单数）车辆自出厂后的行驶里程

6. **impairment** *n.* 损害,损伤

   impair *vi* 损伤

Notes

Fatigue is a form of impairment, so don't give in to that temptation to push on. 疲劳对身体是种伤害,所以不能疲劳驾车。

Key to the Exercises

1. O   2. A   3. C   4. D   5. F   6. G   7. I   8. K   9. M   10. N

Passage 3

> **Directions**
>
> The passage is followed by some questions or unfinished statement. For each of them there are four choices marked A, B, C and D. You should decide on the best choice after reading.

Mountain Climbing

Most young people enjoy some form of physical activity. It may be walking, cycling. swimming, in winter, skating or skiing. It may be game of some kind football, hockey (曲棍球), golf, or tennis. It may be mountaineering.

Those who have a passion for climbing high and difficult mountains are often looked upon with astonishment. Why are men and women willing to suffer cold and hardship, and to take risks on high mountains? This astonishment is caused probably by the difference between mountaineering and other forms of activity to which men give their leisure.

Mountaineering is a sport and not a game. There are no man-made rules, as there are for such games as golf and football. There are, of course, rules of a different kind which it would be dangerous to ignore, but it is this freedom from man-made rules that makes mountaineering attractive to many people. Those who climb mountains are free to use their own methods.

If we compare mountaineering and other more familiar sports, we might think that one big difference is that mountaineering is not a "team game". We should be mistaken in this. There are, it is true, no "matches" between "teams" of climbers, but when climbers are on a rock, face linked by a rope on which their lives may depend, there is obviously teamwork.

The mountain climber knows that he may have to fight forces that are stronger and more powerful than man. He has to fight the forces of nature. His sport requires high mental and physical qualities.

A mountain climber continues to improve in skill year after year. A skier is probably past his best by the age of thirty, and most international tennis champions are in their early twenties. But it is not unusual for man of fifty or sixty to climb the highest mountains in Alps. They may take more time than younger men, but they probably climb with more skill and less waste of effort, and they certainly experience equal enjoyment.

Approximate Length: 336 words

1. Mountaineering is a sport which involves _____.
   A. hardship   B. cold   C. physical risk   D. all the above
2. The main difference between a sport and a game lies in the origin of the _____.
   A. uniform   B. activity   C. rules   D. skills
3. Mountaineering is also a team sport because _____.
   A. it involves rules
   B. it involves matches between teams
   C. it requires mental and physical qualities
   D. mountaineers depend on each other while climbing
4. Which of the following is TRUE?
   A. Mountaineers compete against each other.
   B. Mountaineers compete against teams.
   C. Mountaineers compete against nature.
   D. Mountaineers compete against international standard.
5. What is the best title for the text?
   A. Mountaineering.
   B. Mountain Climbers.
   C. Mountaineering Is Different from Golf and Football.

D. Mountaineering Is More Dangerous than Other Sports.

Words & Expressions

1. **mountaineering** *n.* 登山
2. **passion** *n.* 强烈的情感,激情(尤指性爱、愤怒或对某种思想、原则信念)
3. **leisure** *n.* 空闲,闲暇,安逸
   e. g. a leisure suit 便装
4. **look upon ... with** 用……看待
5. **take risk** 冒险
6. **freedom from** 摆脱约束,不受限制
   e. g. freedom from anxiety 无忧无虑

Notes

1. This astonishment is caused probably by the difference between mountaineering and other forms of activity to which men give their leisure. 这种刺激可能是由于登山运动和人类进行的其他形式休闲活动的差异造成。
2. Those who have a passion for climbing high and difficult mountains are often looked upon with astonishment. 人们对于那些爱好攀登高难度山的人总怀有一种敬畏感。
3. There are, of course, rules of a different kind which it would be dangerous to ignore, but it is this freedom from man-made rules that makes mountaineering attractive to many people. 的确,登山有不同的规则容易被忽视,但是它不受人为规则的约束,从而吸引更多的人。
4. There are, it is true, no "matches" between "teams" of climbers, but when climbers are on a rock, face linked by a rope on which their lives may depend, there is obviously teamwork. 的确,在登山队中没有比赛,然而,在悬崖边当登山者被一条绳子拴在一起决定他们性命的时候,显然这是一种团队工作。

Key to the Exercises

1. D   2. C   3. D   4. C   5. A

Passage 4

Directions

The passage is followed by some questions or unfinished statement. For each of them there are four choices marked A, B, C and D. You should decide on the best choice after reading.

Changes of Society

Social change is more likely to occur in societies where there is a mixture of different kinds of people than in societies where people are similar in many ways. The simple reason for this is that there are more different ways of looking at things present in the first kind of society. There are more ideas, more disagreements in interest, and more groups and organizations with different beliefs. In addition, there is usually a greater worldly interest and greater tolerance in mixed societies. All these factors tend to promote social change by opening more areas of life to decision. In a society where people are quite similar in many ways, there are fewer occasions for people to see the need or the opportunity for change because everything seems to be the same. And although conditions may not be satisfactory, they are at least customary and undisputed.

Within a society, social change is also likely to occur more frequently and more readily in the material aspects of the culture than in the non-material, for example, in technology rather than in values; in what has been learned later in life rather than what was learned early; in the less basic and less emotional aspects of society than in their opposites; in the simple elements rather than in the complex ones; in form rather than in substance; and in elements that are acceptable to the culture rather than in strange elements.

Furthermore, social change is easier if it is gradual. For example, it comes more readily in human relations on a continuous scale rather than one with sharp dichotomies (二分法，一分为二). This is one reason why change has not come more quickly to Black Americans as compared to other American minorities, because of the sharp difference in appearance between them and their white counterparts.

Approximate Length：324 words

1. According to the passage, one of the factors that tend to promote social change is _____.

    A. mutual interest　　　　　　　　B. different points of view

    C. more worldly people　　　　　　D. advanced technology

2. Social change is less likely to occur in a society where people are quite similar in many ways because _____.

A. people there are always satisfied with their living conditions

B. people there have identical needs that can be met without much disputes

C. people there have got accustomed to their conditions that they seldom think it necessary to change

D. people there are less emotional and easy to please

3. According to the passage, which of the following is NOT true?

A. Social values play an important role in social change.

B. Social change is more likely to occur in the material aspects of society.

C. Social change is more likely to occur if it comes gradually.

D. Social change tends to meet with more difficulty in basic and emotional aspects of society.

4. The expression "greater tolerance" in paragraph 1 refers to _____.

A. greater willingness to accept social change

B. quicker adoption to changing circumstances

C. more respect for different beliefs and behavior

D. greater readiness to agree to different opinions and ideas

5. The passage mainly discusses _____.

A. two different societies

B. the necessary of social change

C. different social changes

D. certain factors that determine the ease with which social changes occur

Words & Expressions

1. **disagreements** *n.* 分歧,意见不一致;争论

2. **worldly** *adj.* 世俗的,尘世的;生活经验丰富的,老成练达的

3. **tolerance** *n.* 容忍,忍受

4. **undisputed** *adj.* 无可置疑的;无异议的

   e.g. undisputed answer 无可置疑的答案

5. **minority** *n.* 少数,少数派;(*pl.*) 少数民族

   e.g. be in the minority 占少数

   People from ethnic minorities often face prejudice and discrimination. 来自少数民族的人们常常面临偏见和歧视。

6. **counterpart** *n.* 职位相当的人或物;对等物

   e.g. Belgian officials are discussing this with their French counterparts. 比利时官员与法国同级的官员正在讨论这个问题。

Notes

1. For example, it comes more readily in human relations on a continuous scale rather than one with sharp dichotomies. 例如,社会变化更容易发生在不断变化的人际关系中,而并非尖锐的人际关系中。

2. Social change is more likely to occur in societies where there is a mixture of different kinds of people than in societies where people are similar in many ways. 社会变化更容易发生在有不同种族组成的社会里,而不是在很多方面人们有相似点的社会里。

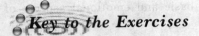

Key to the Exercises

1. B　　2. B　　3. A　　4. A　　5. D

Unit

2

Passage 1

Directions

There are 10 questions after the passage. Go over the passage quickly and answer
the questions in the given time.

For questions 1-7, mark

Y (for YES)   if the statement agrees with the information given in the passage;

N (for NO)   if the statement contradicts the information given in the passage;

NG (for NOT GIVEN) if the information is not given in the passage.

For questions 8 - 10, complete the sentences with the information given in the
passage.

Getting on with Your Kids

Once a parent, always a parent. And yet, as your children grow and evolve, so must
your relationship with them. You need to be supportive but not intrusive; offer emotional
support without being overly involved in their lives; and hope they make wise choices, while
understanding that those choices are theirs to make.

Offering your love and support while respecting your children's choices can help you
build a more enduring relationship with them. The tips below can help you bond with your
kids even though they're no longer kids. And remember: this, too, is a matter of health for
you. For nothing can break your heart as much as a strained or ruined relationship with your
grown child. And nothing can make your heart soar as much as watching their lives prosper
and them wanting you to be an integral part of it.

Set a standing（永久的） dinner date

There's something comforting and secure about the family gathered around the dinner table, perhaps because that tradition is rapidly disappearing. Yet the evening meal is often the one time of day when the family can gather in one place and reinforce their unity. So make dinner a family affair, even if you're sharing takeout at the dinner table. You can use the opportunity to share the news of the day, make weekend plans, and enjoy one another's company. As a bonus, research shows that adolescents who have dinner with their families at least several times a week are less likely to smoke and use drugs and tend to make higher grades.

Back off, but stay close

"It's normal for teens to want to spend more time with friends than parents," says Debbie Glasser, Ph. D. , a licensed clinical psychologist, past chair of the National Parenting Education Network, and founder of News for Parents, a nationally recognized news provider for parents. But don't take this as your cue that your job as a parent is diminished. Find ways to remain involved in your child's life. For example, while your years of volunteering in his classroom may be over, you can still remain involved in his school by joining the PTA or organizing a school fund-raiser. While play dates are a thing of the past, you can still get to know his friends by inviting them to the house after school. "Staying involved during these years may be more challenging now, but it's an important way to enhance your relationship with your child. " says Dr. Glasser.

Share your own feelings with your teen

Of course, spare the intimate details of very personal subjects, but confiding that you, too, occasionally feel angry, insecure, or awkward shows your teenager that you're not just a parent, you're human. Not only will your child feel closer to you, but he or she may feel safe enough to disclose uncomfortable issues or feelings when they arise.

Respect your teen's privacy

Don't read her diary, eavesdrop（偷听） on his phone conversations, or badger her with questions. If their behavior is troubling you, address it directly, using five little words: "Can we talk about it?" Some examples: "I've smelled smoke when you walk into the room several times now. Have you been smoking? Can we talk about it?" or, "You seem very quiet lately, and I'm worried about you. Can we talk about it?"

Trust your children to make smart choices

Of course, they'll make the wrong ones occasionally. But especially if they're over 18, give them the chance to figure out solutions to problems on their own, without interference. After all, didn't you want the same from your parents when you were their age?

Call before you drop by

If you have an adult child, always call before you go to his home, unless it's absolutely necessary. (Do you like it when guests show up on your doorstep uninvited?) If you're the parent of a teen, knock before you enter his room.

Accept their holiday absences with grace

Yes, you may be disappointed that your children—and their children—spend Thanksgiving or Christmas without you. But don't nag or complain about it. You may win a battle over the in-law's house they visit for Christmas, but lose your child's respect and a strong, enduring relationship.

When you catch yourself about to say, "If I were you . . . ", change the subject or leave the room for a moment to collect yourself. Your reward: a closer relationship with a child who appreciates that you respect his autonomy.

Think about the things you value in your other relationships

It's a good bet that trust, respect, and attention top the list, along with shared good time and unconditional acceptance. There you have it: the recipe for the perfect parent-child relationship.

State your views, then invite reaction

"Does that seem fair to you? Can you think of a better way to deal with this? What would you do in my position?" It's easy for a teen to be unreasonable if you take on the burden of reasonableness all by yourself. Share it and they'll find it harder to dismiss your position. Plus, you're more likely to land on middle ground you can both accept.

Be there when they want you or need you, rather than when you want to be

A lifetime of love, trust, and respect will ensue if you are reliably around whenever a reasonable and acceptable request is made of you.

Be honest

Many parents offer praise when they shouldn't, as well as when they should. That just undermines trust. We've all heard, "When you haven't got anything nice to say. . . " But in fact, if both your praise and criticism are heartfelt and valid, your child will learn to trust you.

Cultivate love, but demand respect

This may sound a bit Machiavellian, but Machiavelli may well have been a good dad! Don't try so hard to be your child's friend that you fail to set limits, protect your own integrity, and earn respect. You can be friends long after your child is grown as long as you are the parent first.

Acknowledge that things have changed since you were their age

What they have such as clothes, technology, language, style, educational methods, the job market, even sexual mores and attitudes has evolved significantly in recent years. And the speed of change is only accelerating. You cannot keep up with it all, nor should you. But you do need to strike a balance: Don't live in the past, but don't try to bluff that you know exactly what's going on among teens today either. The middle ground is to live in the present, but your grown-up present. That includes being conversant about the Internet, HDTV, cell phones, the state of the economy, the world marketplace. Your kids will respect you if you are contemporary in a mature way, and don't base your observations of their lives on a past irrelevant to them.

Decode your child's "love language"

While you may love your children dearly, they may not understand the ways you show your love and you may not understand the ways they're best able to receive it. Some children need lots of hugs and cuddles; others may not be as touchy-feely(暴躁的). Some children want you to spend time with them, while others need lots of independence. The next time you spend time with your child, pay attention to the cues he or she sends so you can better interpret the way your child needs to be loved.

> Approximate Length: 1,242 words
> Suggested reading time: 9 minutes
> How fast do you read?＿＿＿＿＿＿

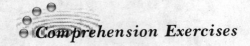

Comprehension Exercises

Complete the following exercises without referring back to the passage you have read.

1. To build a more enduring relationship with children, parents should make decisions for them.

2. Dinner time is a good time for a family to promote family unity.

3. It is easier for parents to get along well with their teens.

4. Parents and children had better tell each other emotional problems.

5. For children's good, parents should monitor children's telephone calls.

6. Don't praise your children when they don't deserve it.

7. Tell your children how to improve their performance in exams.

8. Parents should not _____ about their children's absence on Christmas, or Thanksgiving Day.

9. Children will respect parents if they are contemporary in _____.

10. Although parents love their children very much, they may not know how _____.

Words & Expressions

1. **intrusive** *adj.* 打扰的；插入的

2. **enduring** *adj.* 持久的；持续的

3. **prosper** *vi.* 成功；兴旺；发达

   e.g. prosper in business 生意兴旺发达

4. **integral** *adj.* 构成整体所必需的；不可缺少的

   e.g. Effective communication is an integral part of being a teacher. 有效的沟通技巧是教师不可缺少的。

5. **bonus** *n.* 奖金

6. **adolescent** *adj.* 青春期的，青春的 *n.* 青少年

7. **cue** *n.* 暗示，提示

8. **back off** 逐渐退出

   e.g. He backed off when he realized how much work was involved. 他认识到有多少工作要做之后，便退出了。

9. **confide** *vt.* 吐露（隐私）；托付给某人照管

   e.g. confide in sb. 向某人吐露隐私

10. **badger ... with** 纠缠

11. **undermine** *vt.* 逐渐损坏，逐渐削弱

    e.g. She tried to undermine his reputation. 她企图逐渐损坏他的名声。

12. **Machiavellian** *adj.* 马基雅弗利的，权谋术的 *n.* 权谋政治家

13. **integrity** *n.* 正直，诚实

    e.g. a man of integrity 一个诚实的人

14. **accelerate** *vt.* 加速

    e.g. accelerate the speed 加速

15. **conversant** *adj.* 亲近的；有交情的；熟悉的

16. **contemporary** *adj.* 当代的

Notes

1. PTA—Parent-Teacher Association：家庭教师协会

2. HDTV—High-Definition TV：高清晰度电视

3. But you do need to strike a balance. 但是你的确要公平对待。

4. Your kids will respect you if you are contemporary in a mature way, and don't base your observations of their lives on a past irrelevant to them. 孩子们会尊重你,只要你能跟上时代,而不是用过去的眼光来认识孩子们的生活。

5. Machiavelli 马基雅弗利(意大利新兴资产阶级思想政治家,历史学家)

Key to the Exercises

1. N　　2. Y　　3. N　　4. Y　　5. N　　6. Y　　7. NG

8. nag and complain　　9. a mature way　　10. to show their love

Passage　2

Directions

In this section, there is a passage with 10 blanks. You are required to select one word for each blank from a list of choices given in a word bank following the passage. Read the passage through carefully before making your choices. Each choice in the bank is identified by a letter. Please choose the corresponding letter for each item. You may not use any of the words in the bank more than once.

Writers and Railways

　　Nineteenth-century writers in the United States, whether they wrote novels, short stories, poems, or plays, were powerfully drawn to the railroad in its __1__ year. In fact, writers __2__ to the railroads as soon as the first was built in the 1830's. By the 1850's, the railroad was a __3__ presence in the life of the nation. Writers such as Ralph Waldo Emerson and Henry David Thoreau saw the railroad both as a boon to democracy and as an object of

___4___. The railroad could be and was a despoiler of nature; furthermore, in its manifestation of speed and noise, it might be a despoiler of human nature as well. By the 1850's and 1860's, there was a great ___5___ among writers and intellectuals of the rapid industrialization of which the railroad was a leading force. Deeply philosophical historians such as Henry Adams lamented the role that the new frenzy for business was playing in eroding traditional values. A distrust of industry and business continued among writers ___6___ the rest of the nineteenth century and into the twentieth. For the most part, the ___7___ in which the railroad plays an important role belongs to popular culture rather than to the realm of serious art. One thinks of melodramas, boys' books, thrillers, romances, and the like rather than novels of the first rank. In the railroads' prime years, between 1890 and 1920, there were a few individuals in the United States, most of them with solid railroading experience behind them, who made a ___8___ of writing about railroading—works offering the ambience (环境,气氛) of stations, yards, and locomotive cabs. These writers, who can ___9___ be said to have created a genre, the "railroad novels" are now mostly forgotten, their names having faded from memory. But anyone who takes the time to consult their fertile writings will still find a ___10___ trove (发现的东西) of information about the place of the railroad in the lift of the United States.

Approximate Length: 324 words

A. golden   B. admission   C. responded

D. major   E. ambition   F. suspicion

G. beyond   H. distrust   I. apparently

J. throughout   K. literature   L. perceived

M. profession   N. genuinely   O. treasure

1. _____   2. _____   3. _____   4. _____   5. _____

6. _____   7. _____   8. _____   9. _____   10. _____

Words & Expressions

1. **boon** *n.* 恩惠,实惠,福利

2. **despoiler** *n.* 抢夺者,剥夺者

3. **manifestation** *n.* 说明,展示

4. **lament** *vt.* 痛惜,为……悲哀;抱怨

   e. g. The nation lamented the death of the great leader. 全国为他们的伟大领袖之死而悲哀。

5. **frenzy** *n.* 狂暴,狂怒

6. **realm** *n.* (知识、兴趣、思想的)领域

e. g. the spiritual realm 精神领域

7. **thriller** *n.* 惊险小说；惊险电影

8. **prime** *adj.* 最重要的；首要的

   e. g. Smoking is the prime cause of heart disease. 抽烟是引发心脏病的首要原因。

9. **genre** *n.* （正式）艺术、写作、音乐等的类型；体裁

Notes

1. Ralph Waldo Emerson：美国 19 世纪著名哲学家、文学家。

2. Henry David Thoreau：19 世纪最广为人知的美国作家之一。也许只有埃德加·爱伦·坡（Edgar Allan Poe）才能与之相比。后人把他们当做那个时代反主流文化的代表人物。

Key to the Exercises

1. A   2. C   3. D   4. F   5. H   6. J   7. K   8. M   9. N   10. O

Passage 3

> **Directions**
>
> The passage is followed by some questions or unfinished statement. For each of them there are four choices marked A, B, C and D. You should decide on the best choice after reading.

Noah Webster and His Dictionary

Noah Webster, one of the founding fathers of America, was born in the village of West Hartford, Connecticut on October 16, 1758. He was a descendant of William Bradford, governor of the Plymouth Colony. Noah graduated from Yale College, studied law, and practiced it for a short time before deciding upon a career in teaching.

It was while teaching at school that Noah sought to fulfill his calling and use his talents to the betterment of the educational system of the newly formed Republic. He sought to build an educational system embracing the "love of virtue, patriotism, and religion." He believed that "education was useless without the Bible." Mr. Webster wrote, "in my view, the Christian religion is one of the first things in which all children ought to be instructed."

In 1780, while teaching at school, he compiled *The Blue-Backed Speller*, an elementary spelling book, which sold well into the millions. Noah also compiled grammar books, readers, literature books, American history texts, etc. In his textbooks he promoted Christian character building and patriotism.

Noah Webster, though accomplishing great works for early America, had another dream. He one day hoped to present to his country the first American dictionary. After many painstaking years of research and study, learning twenty languages, and with the encouragement of Benjamin Franklin, James Madison, and other American leaders, Noah Webster completed the first American dictionary. It was published in 1828 in two volumes, entitled *The American Dictionary of the English Language*.

Webster recorded the entire manuscript of the dictionary by hand. The volume of words exceeded all others, with the total number of words defined reaching 70,000. This included 12,000 new words and 40,000 new definitions never before printed in a dictionary. He held to high Christian standards, refusing to admit vulgarism and slang into America's first dictionary. Noah Webster's 1828 dictionary surpassed all others of his day and became a mark of excellence to the new republic.

Approximate Length: 321 words

1. Noah Webster's first job was _____.
   A. teaching   B. compiling dictionary
   C. building an educational system   D. practicing law
2. Noah Webster hoped that through education _____.
   A. students could learn to love virtue, patriotism and religion
   B. all people could get well educated
   C. students could develop comprehensively
   D. students could become Christians
3. One of Noah Webster's dreams was _____.
   A. writing more books for Americans   B. compiling an American dictionary
   C. educating all Americans   D. promoting patriotism
4. Which of the following is NOT true?
   A. Webster's research and study got the encouragement of many American leaders.
   B. The entire manuscript of the dictionary was recorded by hand.
   C. The dictionary included new words, new definitions and some slang.
   D. Because of the dictionary, Webster was regarded as one of the founding fathers of

America.

5. The best title of the passage could be _____.

A. Noah Webster and His Dictionary   B. Noah Webster and American Education

C. The First American Dictionary   D. Webster and His Teaching Career

Words & Expressions

1. **Hartford** *n.* 哈特福德（美国康涅狄格州首府）

2. **Connecticut** *n.* 康涅狄格州

3. **descendant** *n.* 子孙后代

   e.g. Chinese descendants 华裔后代

4. **Plymouth** *n.* 普利茅斯（英国港口城市）

5. **patriotism** *n.* 爱国主义

   e.g. cultivate patriotism 培养爱国主义

6. **painstaking** *n&adj.* 辛苦；辛勤的，艰苦的

   e.g. a painstaking investigation 艰苦的调查

7. **embrace** *v&n.* 拥抱；包含；信奉

   e.g. embrace each other warmly 热情拥抱对方；embrace Buddhism 信奉佛教

8. **sought**（**pt and pp of seek**）*vt.* 寻求，探索

   e.g. seek to find a way out 寻求一条出路

9. **compile** *vt.* 编纂

   e.g. compile a dictionary 编纂一部词典

10. **vulgarism** *n.* 粗俗

Notes

1. Noah graduated from Yale College, studied law, and practiced it for a short time before deciding upon a career in teaching. 诺亚毕业于耶鲁大学的法律专业，在他决定从事教育事业之前曾短期供职于法律系统。

2. He sought to build an educational system embracing the "love of virtue, patriotism, and religion". 他探索要建立一个重视"美德、爱国主义、宗教"的教育体制。

3. In his textbooks he promoted Christian character building and patriotism. 在他的课本里，他倡导基督教徒性格的塑造和爱国主义的培养。

4. He one day hoped to present to his country the first American dictionary. 他希望有一天能够向他的国家呈现第一部美国词典。

5. After many painstaking years of research and study, learning twenty languages, and with the encouragement of Benjamin Franklin, James Madison, and other American leaders, Noah Webster completed the first American dictionary. 由于多年的苦心研究和学会了20种语

言,再加上本杰明・弗兰克林、詹姆斯・麦迪逊及其他美国领导的鼓励,诺亚・韦伯斯特终于完成了美国第一部词典。

6. He held to high Christian standards, refusing to admit vulgarism and slang into America's first dictionary. 他笃信基督教的信条,拒绝在他的第一部词典里介绍粗俗语和俚语。

Key to the Exercises

1. D　　　2. A　　　3. B　　　4. C　　　5. A

Passage　4

Directions

The passage is followed by some questions or unfinished statement. For each of them there are four choices marked A, B, C and D. You should decide on the best choice after reading.

IQ and EQ

It has been proved time and again in that good marks at school do not guarantee a successful life. Other factors like social class, luck (not everyone may agree) also have their own roles to play.

EQ is a relatively new concept. It is the capacity for our own feelings and those of others, for motivating ourselves, and for managing emotions well in ourselves and in our relationships. Emotional intelligence describes abilities distinct from but complementary to IQ. Many people who are book smart but lack emotional intelligence end up working for people who have lower IQ. Just like mathematics or reading, the world of emotions is an area that can be mastered more or less skillfully and requires mental alertness. Upon mapping we realize that EQ is a special capacity, which determines how well we are able to make use of the other skills that we possess, besides IQ.

People with good emotional capacity know their feelings well and are in control of them; they can read other people's feelings and deal with them effectively. These people have an advantage over others in all aspects of life, be it professional or personal. People with this intelligence have a defined thinking process, which in turn promotes productivity.

People, who are not in control of their emotions, fight internal struggles that inhibit their ability to think clearly and concentrate on their work. This is the main reason why people start looking for new jobs or are dissatisfied with the way their present company is treating them. It is their emotional intelligence that is failing them. What such people need is not another job but mastery over their own world of emotions.

It is emotional intelligence that motivates us to pursue our unique potential and purpose, and activates our innermost values and aspirations, transforming them from things we think about to what we live.

Approximate Length: 313 words

1. It is the author's opinion that _____.
   A. good marks do not promise a success in one's life
   B. social class influences one's success
   C. good marks play bigger role than luck
   D. luck may determine one's success

2. A person who is "book smart" (Line 5, Para. 2) is one who _____.
   A. is quick to learn   B. is sensitive to books
   C. is a book worm   D. becomes smart after reading a book

3. People with good emotional capacity _____.
   A. know to take advantage of others
   B. can do the right thing at the right time
   C. are professionally successful
   D. know their own feelings as well as those of others

4. According to the passage, those looking for new jobs _____.
   A. find new jobs more interesting   B. need to learn how to control their emotions
   C. find new jobs more challenging   D. indeed need a new job

5. From the tone of the passage we can say that the author _____.
   A. prefers to have high IQ
   B. objects to high IQ
   C. believes IQ and EQ are equally important
   D. advocates EQ

Words & Expressions

1. **EQ** *n.* emotional quotient 情商

2. **capacity** *n.* 能力

   e.g. capacity for finding strong points in others 在别人身上发现优点的能力

3. **motivate** *vt.* 激发

   e.g. be motivated by love，fear，greed 受爱(恐惧、贪婪等的)驱使

4. **distinct** *adj.* 清楚的,截然不同的

   e.g. be distinct from something else 与……截然不同

5. **complementary** *adj.* 补充的,补足的

   e.g. be complementary to something else 补充……

6. **end up** 以……而结束

   e.g. end up being a loser 以一个失败者而结束

7. **have an advantage over** 有……优势

8. **inhibit** *vt.* 抑制,约束;使羞于

   e.g. inhibit the wide spread of the disease 抑制疾病的传播

9. **aspiration** *n.* 渴望

   e.g. aspiration for knowledge 渴望知识

10. **transform** *vt.* 转换,改变

    e.g. transform something from...to... 把……从……转换成……

 *Notes*

1. It has been proved time and again in that good marks at school do not guarantee a successful life. 已经多次证实,在学校里考试得高分并不能够保证一个人将来就会拥有成功的人生。

2. It is the capacity for our own feelings and those of others，for motivating ourselves，and for managing emotions well in ourselves and in our relationships. 情商是一种处理自己和他人感受的能力,它能激发我们有效地控制自己的情绪和处理与他人的关系。

3. Many people who are book smart but lack emotional intelligence end up working for people who have lower IQ. 好多擅长读书、智商高而缺乏情商的人最终却在为那些比自己智商低的人工作。

4. Upon mapping we realize that EQ is a special capacity，which determines how well we are able to make use of the other skills that we possess，besides IQ. 我们应当意识到情商是一种特殊的能力,它决定了我们能够在多大程度上充分利用自身除了智商之外的其他技能。

5. People with good emotional capacity know their feelings well and are in control of them；they can read other people's feelings and deal with them effectively. 拥有高情商的人很熟悉自己的感受并且能控制自己的情绪;他们能够读懂他人的感受并能与他人很好地相处。

6. People，who are not in control of their emotions，fight internal struggles that inhibit their ability to think clearly and concentrate on their work. 那些控制不了自身情绪的人,内心深处充满了矛盾斗争,而这些矛盾又会使自己不能认真思考、集中精力地工作。

7. It is emotional intelligence that motivates us to pursue our unique potential and purpose，and activates our innermost values and aspirations，transforming them from things we

think about to what we live. 情商促使我们发掘自身独特的潜能和决心,它激发我们内心最深处的价值观念和渴望,并将它们从意念中转换成为我们毕生所要追求的目标。

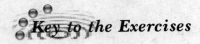
Key to the Exercises

1. A   2. A   3. D   4. B   5. D

Passage 1

Ozone and Your Health

On a hot, smoggy summer day, have you ever wondered: Is the air safe to breathe? Should I be concerned about going outside?

In fact, breathing smoggy air can be hazardous because smog contains ozone, a pollutant that can harm our health when there are elevated levels in the air we breathe.

What is ozone?

Ozone is a colorless gas composed of three atoms of oxygen. Ozone occurs both in the Earth's upper atmosphere and at ground level. Ozone can be good or bad, depending on where it is found.

Good Ozone. Ozone occurs naturally in the Earth's upper atmosphere—10 to 30 miles above the Earth's surface where it forms a protective layer that shields us from the sun's harmful ultraviolet rays. This "good" ozone is gradually being destroyed by manmade chemicals. An area where ozone has been most significantly depleted, for example, over the North or South pole is sometimes called a "hole in the ozone."

Bad Ozone. In the Earth's lower atmosphere, near ground level, ozone is formed when pollutants emitted by cars, power plants, industrial boilers, refineries, chemical plants, and other sources react chemically in the presence of sunlight.

How might ozone affect my health?

Scientists have been studying the effects of ozone on human health for many years. So far, they have found that ozone can cause several types of short-term health effects in the lungs.

Ozone can irritate the respiratory system. When this happens, you might start coughing, feel an irritation in your throat, and experience an uncomfortable sensation in your chest. These symptoms can last for a few hours after ozone exposure and may even become painful.

Ozone can reduce lung function. When scientists refer to "lung function," they mean the volume of air that you draw in when you take a full breath and the speed at which you are able to blow it out. Ozone can make it more difficult for you to breathe as deeply and vigorously as you normally would. When this happens, you may notice that breathing starts to feel uncomfortable. If you are exercising or working outdoors, you may notice that you are taking more rapid and shallow breaths than normal. Reduced lung function can be a particular problem for outdoor workers, competitive athletes, and other people who exercise outdoors.

Ozone can aggravate asthma (哮喘). When ozone levels are high, more asthmatics have asthma attacks that require a doctor's attention or the use of additional medication. One reason this happens is that ozone makes people more sensitive to allergens (［医］过敏原), which are the most common triggers for asthma attacks. Also, asthmatics are more severely affected by the reduced lung function and irritation that ozone causes in the respiratory system.

Ozone can inflame and damage the lining of the lung. Some scientists have compared ozone's effect on the lining of the lung to the effect of sunburn on the skin. Ozone damages the cells that line the air spaces in the lung. Within a few days, the damaged cells are replaced and the old cells are shed, much in the way that skin peels after a sunburn. If this kind of damage occurs repeatedly, the lung may change permanently in a way that could cause long-term health effects and a lower quality of life.

Scientists suspect that ozone may have other effects on people's health. Ozone may aggravate chronic lung diseases, such as emphysema (气肿,肺气肿) and bronchitis. Also, studies in animals suggest that ozone may reduce the immune system's ability to fight off bacterial infections in the respiratory system.

Most of these effects are considered to be short-term effects because they eventually cease once the individual is no longer exposed to elevated levels of ozone. However, scientists are concerned that repeated short-term damage from ozone exposure may permanently injure the lung. For example, repeated ozone impacts on the developing lungs of children may lead to reduced lung function as adults. Also, ozone exposure may speed up the decline in lung function that occurs as a natural result of the aging process. Research is under way to help us better understand the possible long-term effects of ozone exposure.

Who is most at risk from ozone?

Four groups of people, described below, are particularly sensitive to ozone. These groups become sensitive to ozone when they are active outdoors, because physical activity (such as jogging or outdoor work) causes people to breathe faster and more deeply. During activity, ozone penetrates deeper into the parts of the lungs that are more vulnerable to injury. Sensitive groups include:

Children. Active children are the group at highest risk from ozone exposure. Such children often spend a large part of their summer vacation outdoors, engaged in vigorous activities either in their neighborhood or at summer camp. Children are also more likely to have asthma or other respiratory illnesses. Asthma is the most common chronic disease for children and may be aggravated by ozone exposure.

Adults who are active outdoors. Healthy adults of all ages who exercise or work vigorously outdoors are considered a "sensitive group" because they have a higher level of exposure to ozone than people who are less active outdoors.

People with respiratory diseases, such as asthma. There is no evidence that ozone causes asthma or other chronic respiratory disease, but these diseases do make the lungs more vulnerable to the effects of ozone. Thus, individuals with these conditions will generally experience the effects of ozone earlier and at lower levels than less sensitive individuals.

People with unusual susceptibility to ozone. Scientists don't yet know why, but some healthy people are simply more sensitive to ozone than others. These individuals may experience more health effects from ozone exposure than the average person.

Scientists have studied other groups to find out whether they are at increased risk from ozone. So far there is little evidence to suggest that either the elderly or people with heart disease have heightened sensitivity to ozone. However, like other adults, elderly people will be at higher risk from ozone exposure if they suffer from respiratory disease, are active outdoors, or are unusually susceptible to ozone as described above.

How can I tell if I am being affected by ozone?

Often, people exposed to ozone experience recognizable symptoms, including coughing, irritation in the airways, rapid or shallow breathing, and discomfort when breathing or general discomfort in the chest. People with asthma may experience asthma attacks. When ozone levels are higher than normal, any of these symptoms may indicate that you should minimize the time spent outdoors, or at least reduce your activity level, to protect your health until ozone levels decline.

Ozone damage can also occur without any noticeable signs. Sometimes there are no symptoms, or sometimes they are too subtle to notice. People who live in areas where ozone levels are frequently high may find that their initial symptoms of ozone exposure go away over time, particularly when exposure to high ozone levels continues for several days. This does not mean that they have developed resistance to ozone. In fact, scientists have found that ozone continues to cause lung damage even when the symptoms have disappeared. The best way to protect your health is to find out when ozone levels are elevated in your area and take simple precautions to minimize exposure even when you don't feel obvious symptoms.

How do scientists know about the health effects of ozone?

EPA has gathered a great deal of information about the health effects of ozone. This information comes from a number of sources, including animal research, studies that compare health statistics and ozone levels within communities, and controlled testing of human volunteers to determine how ozone affects lung function. In these studies, volunteers are exposed to ozone in specially designed chambers where their responses can be carefully measured. Volunteers are prescreened in medical examinations to determine their health status, and they are never exposed to ozone levels that exceed those found in major cities on a very smoggy day.

Though our understanding of ozone's effects has increased substantially in recent years, many important questions still remain to be investigated. For example, does repeated short-term exposure to high levels of ozone cause permanent lung damage? Does repeated exposure during childhood to high levels of ozone cause reduced lung function in adults? Scientists are continuing to study these and other questions to gain a better understanding of ozone's effects.

Approximate Length: 1,067 words
Suggested reading time: 9 minutes
How fast do you read? _____

Comprehension Exercises

Complete the following exercises without referring back to the passage you have read.

1. Ozone exists only high above the atmosphere.
2. Ozone can protect people from harmful rays from space.
3. Robots can not be affected by Ozone.

4. Asthma is caused by ozone.

5. People working indoors are more likely to be harmed by ozone.

6. There is no evidence that how ozone affects people with heart diseases.

7. People sensitive to ozone are more easily to be affected by ozone.

8. Ozone is a colorless gas consisting of _____.

9. Scientists have found that ozone can cause several types of _____ in the lungs.

10. Ozone can be _____, depending on where it is found.

Words & Expressions

1. **ozone** *n.* 臭氧

2. **hazardous** *adj.* 危险的

3. **elevate** *vt.* 增加,提高;提升,晋升;使情绪高昂

   e.g. These drugs may elevate acid levels in the blood. 这些药可能会增加血液酸度。

4. **ultraviolet** *adj.* 紫外线的

5. **deplete** *v.* (使)耗尽(一般用被动语态)

   e.g. Our food reserves had been severely depleted over the winter. 经过一冬天,我们的食物储备已经消耗的差不多了。

6. **refinery** *n.* (金属、糖或石油的)提炼厂

   e.g. an oil refinery 炼油厂

7. **aggravate** *vt.* 使恶化,加重

   e.g. Poor living conditions aggravate his illness. 贫困的生活条件加重了他的病情。

8. **susceptibility** *n.* 易感性,感受性,感情

9. **respiratory disease** 呼吸系统疾病

10. **sunburn** *n.* 晒伤;皮肤灼痛

11. **immune** *adj.* 对疾病有免疫力的

    e.g. be immune to 对……有免疫的;不受……影响的

12. **vulnerable** *adj.* 易受伤害的,脆弱的;易受攻击的

    e.g. a vulnerable young child 易受伤害的小孩

Notes

1. EPA—Environmental Protection Agency：美国环保署

2. Ozone can inflame and damage the lining of the lung. 臭氧可以损坏肺的内壁。

3. People who live in areas where ozone levels are frequently high may find that their initial symptoms of ozone exposure go away over time, particularly when exposure to high ozone levels continues for several days. 生活在臭氧含量高地区的人也许发现,过些时间后,他们最初由臭氧引起的症状消失了,尤其是连续几天暴露在含量高的空气后。

Key to the Exercises

1. N 2. Y 3. NG 4. N 5. N 6. Y 7. Y

8. three atoms of oxygen 9. short-term health effects 10. good or bad

Passage 2

Directions

In this section, there is a passage with 10 blanks. You are required to select one word for each blank from a list of choices given in a word bank following the passage. Read the passage through carefully before making your choices. Each choice in the bank is identified by a letter. Please choose the corresponding letter for each item. You may not use any of the words in the bank more than once.

Pearl S. Buck—a Popular American Writer

One of the most popular literary figures in American literature is a woman who spent almost half of her long life in China, a country on a ___1___ thousands of miles from the United States. In her lifetime she earned this country's most ___2___ acclaimed literary award: the Pulitzer Prize, and also the most ___3___ form of literary recognition in the world, the Nobel Prize for Literature. Pearl S. Buck was almost a household word throughout much of her lifetime because of her prolific literary output, which ___4___ of some eighty-five published works, including several dozen novels, six ___5___ of short stories, fourteen books for children, and more than a dozen works of nonfiction. When she was eighty years old, some twenty-five volumes were ___6___ publication. Many of those books were set in China, the land in which she spent so much of her life. Her books and her life served as a ___7___ between the cultures of the East and the West. As the product of those two cultures she became "mentally bifocal." Her unique background made her into an unusually interesting and versatile human being. As we examine the life of Pearl Buck, we cannot help but be ___8___ that we are in fact meeting three separate people: a wife and mother, an internationally famous writer and a humanitarian and philanthropist. One cannot really get to know Pearl Buck without learning about each of the three. Though ___9___ in her lifetime with the William Dean Howell Medal of the American Academy of Arts and Letters in addition to the Nobel and Pulitzer prizes, Pearl Buck as a total human being, not only a famous author, is a __10__ subject of study.

Approximate Length: 285 words

A. bridge   B. captivating   C. investment
D. highly   E. continent   F. appetite
G. romantic   H. aware   I. consisted
J. honored   K. collections   L. consequence
M. sophisticated   N. prestigious   O. awaiting

1. _____   2. _____   3. _____   4. _____   5. _____
6. _____   7. _____   8. _____   9. _____   10. _____

Words & Expressions

1. **acclaim** *n.* 喝彩，欢呼；*vt.* 欢呼，称赞

   e. g. His last play was acclaimed by the critics as a masterpiece. 他的最后一部戏剧被评论家誉为他的杰作。

2. **prolific** *adj.* 多产的；丰富的；大量繁殖的

3. **nonfiction** *n.* 非小说类文学作品，写实作品

   fiction *n.* 小说

4. **versatile** *adj.* 通用的，万能的；多才多艺的，多面手的

5. **humanitarian** *adj.* 博爱的；人道主义的

   e. g. humanitarian aid to the refugees 向难民提供的人道主义援助

6. **philanthropist** *n.* 慈善家

Notes

1. the Pulitzer Prize：普利策奖

   美国一种多项的新闻和文化艺术奖金。由美国著名记者和报纸经营人约瑟夫·普利策创立。普利策生前立下遗嘱，将财产捐赠给哥伦比亚大学，设立普利策奖，奖励新闻界、文学界、音乐界的卓越人士。自 1917 年以来每年颁发一次。

2. Pearl S. Buck：赛珍珠（1892—1973）

   她出生于美国弗吉尼亚州，3 个月大时即被身为传教士的双亲带到中国。在双语环境中长大，是以中文为母语之一的著名美国作家。曾回美国 4 年接受高等教育。自 1919—1935 年，她与丈夫卜凯（J. L. Buck）长期居住在所执教的金陵大学分配给他们的两层楼房里。在那里她写出了于 1938 年荣获诺贝尔文学奖的长篇小说《大地三部曲》，她是最早将《水浒传》翻译成英文在西方出版的作家。一生著译作品 70 余部。她病逝后，按其遗愿，墓碑上只镌刻"赛珍珠"三个汉字。

Key to the Exercises

1. E　2. D　3. N　4. I　5. K　6. O　7. A　8. H　9. J　10. B

Passage 3

Directions

The passage is followed by some questions or unfinished statement. For each of them there are four choices marked A, B, C and D. You should decide on the best choice after reading.

Job-hunting Tips

In any market the person with the product best suited to the customer's needs gets the business, and this is also true of job hunting. In the job search, you are the product. So the first thing to do is to define precisely what you have to offer. At this stage, it does not need to be in relation to any particular job; simply put down what your qualifications are, what jobs you have done, how your salary progressed and what you achieved in each job. The last of these is most important and should, as far as possible, be stated clearly. The fact that you were sales manager with a certain company is much less interesting to a would-be employer than the contribution you made while you were there. There is, of course, more to job hunting than just the work content. What are your salary expectations? It is never a good idea to go for jobs that pay significantly less than you are currently earning, because employers are wary of applicants who take a salary drop on the grounds that they either try very hard or will be off at the first better paid opportunity. On the other hand, a perfectly good reason may exist where a change of job direction involves learning new skills. Last, the question of age. It is the one that worries employers more than any other. To be frank, it does get harder to move jobs as you get older, partly because of the complications of transferring pension schemes, but if you have an impressive enough record or valuable enough qualifications, age is not something to be afraid of. Furthermore, though job advertisements do set out age ranges for applicants, employers are not usually worried if you do not fall exactly within them, provided there are other good factors. As anyone who has done any interviewing will tell you, it is very rare to find the applicant who meets all the requirements.

Approximate Length: 329 words

1. To find a new job, one must first of all have a clear understanding of _____.
   A. the position he will be applying for
   B. the characteristics of the present job market
   C. his own ability to do the job well
   D. what he really wants to achieve in life

2. According to the passage, what matters most to an employer is _____.
   A. the applicant's educational background
   B. the applicant's enthusiasm for the new job
   C. the actual contributions the applicant made in his work
   D. the applicant's experience in the job he applies for

3. Applicants who take a salary drop are less likely to be employed except when _____.
   A. the new job involves learning new skills
   B. the applicant needs the new job badly
   C. the new job shows brilliant future
   D. the applicant impresses the employers deeply with his sincerity

4. According to the passage, to employers, the most worrying factor in choosing an applicant is his _____.
   A. experience   C. qualifications   B. contributions   D. age

5. Older applicants also stand a good chance to find new jobs because _____.
   A. many companies prefer to employ people with lots of experience
   B. older applicants usually ask for lower salaries
   C. perfect employees are hard to find today
   D. older employees tend to have a stronger sense of responsibility

Words & Expressions

1. **qualification** *n.* 资格；条件，限制，限定；赋予资格
2. **on the grounds that ...** 理由是……
   e.g. The company fired him on the grounds that he was always late for work. 公司解雇了他，理由是他总是迟到。
3. **be wary of** 提防
   e.g. Be wary of the tiger. 小心那只老虎。
4. **transfer** *vt.* 转移，调转，调任，传递；转让；改变
   e.g. He was transferred from Beijing to Shanghai. 他从北京调到了上海。

5. **pension** *n.* 退休金;抚恤金

　　e.g. He lives on pensions now. 他现在靠退休金生活。

6. **scheme** *n.* 计划,规划,方案;阴谋,诡计

Notes

1. In any market the person with the product best suited to the customer's needs gets the business, and this is also true of job hunting. 在任何市场,拥有最适合消费者需求产品的人才有生意做,找工作也如此。

2. As anyone who has done any interviewing will tell you, it is very rare to find the applicant who meets all the requirements. 任何从事过招工面试的人都会讲,符合招工所有要求的求职者是很少见的。

Key to the Exercises

1. C　　　2. C　　　3. A　　　4. D　　　5. C

Passage 4

Directions

The passage is followed by some questions or unfinished statement. For each of them there are four choices marked A, B, C and D. You should decide on the best choice after reading.

Confusing Measurements

　　A long time ago, when ancient Rome was still an empire, people of that time used the same weights and measures. The standards of those weights and measures were found by the Romans, who kept these standards in a temple in Rome. All standards for measuring weight or distance were the same, whether in Spain or in Syria. But then the Rome Empire fell, and these standards disappeared. Today, standards are different from place to place throughout the world.

Tourists who drive from the United States into Canada, for example, are surprised when they buy gas for their cars. A gallon of gas costs more than they are used to paying. They complain that prices are much higher in Canada than in the United States. Then they discover that they can drive farther on a Canadian gallon than on a United States gallon. Is it a different kind of gas? No, it is different kind of gallon. Canada uses the British gallon that is about one fifth larger than the United States gallon.

Four quarts equal a gallon and two pints equal a quart in both countries. But Canadian quarts and pints are larger than quarts and pints in the United States. The gallon equals 277. 42 cubic inches, while the gallon in the United States is equal to 231 cubic inches. Measured in ounces, Canadian larger gallon holds 160 fluid ounces, while the smaller United States gallon holds no more than 128 fluid ounces. From these figures, it is easy to see why Americans can drive farther on the Canadian gallon than on the American gallon.

Some day, countries may follow the example of the ancient Romans and make weights and measures the same for every nation.

Approximate Length: 286 words

1. The whole passage tells about _____.
   A. the standards for weights and measures found by Romans
   B. the gallon in Canada and the United States
   C. surprised tourists in Canada
   D. the larger American gallon

2. The British gallon is about _____ larger than the United States gallon.
   A. 277. 42 cubic inches   B. 160 fluid ounces
   C. 128 fluid ounces   D. 1/5

3. Which statement does the passage lead you to believe?
   A. It would be good to use the same measure in the whole world.
   B. The Americans hate the Canadian gas.
   C. The Canadian gas is better than that of the United States.
   D. Buying gas in Canada is more expensive than in the United States.

4. Six United States gallons of liquid is about _____ British gallons of liquid.
   A. seven   B. four   C. five   D. three

5. After reading this passage, you can have an impression that _____.
   A. different measures can be a problem
   B. people like different measures
   C. there are all kinds of measures in the world
   D. Americans should not travel too much

Words & Expressions

1. **weights and measures** *n.* 度量衡单位

   e. g. unify weights and measures 统一度量衡标准

2. **temple** *n.* 神殿，寺庙

   e. g. Shaolin Temple 少林寺

3. **Syria** *n.* 叙利亚共和国（西南亚国家）

4. **gallon** *n.* 加仑（容量单位）

5. **quart** *n.* 夸脱（容量单位）

6. **pint** *n.* 品脱（容量单位）

7. **fluid** *n & adj.* 流动性，流动；流动的，不固定的

Notes

1. The standards of those weights and measures were found by the Romans, who kept these standards in a temple in Rome. 度量衡标准是由罗马人定制的，他们把这些度量衡标准保存在罗马一个神殿里。

2. Today, standards are different from place to place throughout the world. 如今，全世界各个地方的度量衡标准各不相同。

3. Then they discover that they can drive farther on a Canadian gallon than on a United States gallon. 后来，他们发现在加拿大加 1 加仑的油跑的路程比美国 1 加仑油跑的路程多。

4. Canada uses the British gallon that is about one fifth larger than the United States gallon. 加拿大用的是英国加仑，比美国 1 加仑约多 1/5 的量。

5. From these figures, it is easy to see why Americans can drive farther on the Canadian gallon than on the American gallon. 从这些数据不难看出，为什么美国人加加拿大 1 加仑的油量比美国 1 加仑的油跑的远。

6. Some day, countries may follow the example of the ancient Romans and make weights and measures the same for every nation. 也许将来的某一天，各国会效仿古罗马人将每一个民族的度量衡标准统一起来，使用一样的标准。

Key to the Exercises

1. B　　2. D　　3. A　　4. C　　5. A

Passage 1

Directions

There are 10 questions after the passage. Go over the passage quickly and answer
the questions in the given time.

For questions 1 – 7, mark

Y (for YES)   if the statement agrees with the information given in the passage;

N (for NO)   if the statement contradicts the information given in the passage;

NG (for NOT GIVEN) if the information is not given in the passage.

For questions 8 – 10, complete the sentences with the information given in the
passage.

Drinking and Driving: Precautions You Can Take

Protect yourself

While society has done much to improve highway safety, you can do much to protect
yourself.

Don't drink and drive and don't ride with anyone who has too much to drink.
Remember, it is usually themselves and their passengers who are harmed by drunk drivers.
The risk of collision for drinking drivers is several hundred times higher than for a non-
drinking driver.

Volunteer to be a designated driver.

Always use a safety seat belt.

Use four-lane highways whenever possible.

Avoid rural roads.

Avoid travel after midnight (especially on Fridays and Saturdays).

Drive defensively.

Choose vehicles with airbags.

Refer to safety ratings before selecting your next vehicle. "Buying a Safer Car" includes safety ratings of cars, vans, and sport utility vehicles by year, make, and model.

Never use illegal drugs. Illicit drugs are involved in a large proportion of traffic fatalities.

Never drive when fatigued. The dangers posed when fatigued are similar to those when intoxicated. A drunk or fatigued driver has slowed reactions and impaired judgment. And a driver who nods off at the wheel has no reactions and no judgment! Drivers who drift off cause about 72,500 injuries and deaths every year.

Don't use a car phone, put on make-up, comb your hair, or eat while driving. Drivers using cellular phones are four times more likely to have an accident than other drivers.

Steer clear of aggressive drivers. Aggressive drivers may be responsible for more deaths than drunk drivers.

If you must drive after drinking, stay completely sober

Don't be fooled. The contents of the typical bottle or can of beer, glass of wine, or liquor drink (mixed drink or straight liquor) each contain virtually identical amounts of pure alcohol.

Know your limit. If you are not sure, experiment at home with your spouse or some other responsible individual. Explain what you are attempting to learn. Most people find that they can consume one drink per hour without any ill effects.

Eat food while you drink. Food, especially high protein food such as meat, cheese and peanuts, will help slow the absorption of alcohol into your body.

Sip your drink. If you gulp a drink, you lose the pleasure of savoring its flavors and aromas (香气，香味). Don't participate in drinking games.

Accept a drink only when you really want one. If someone tries to force a drink on you, ask for a non-alcohol beverage instead. If that doesn't work, "lose" your drink by setting it down somewhere and leaving it.

Skip a drink now and then. Having a non-alcoholic drink between alcoholic ones will help keep your blood alcohol content level down, as does spacing out your alcoholic drinks.

A good general guideline for most people is to limit consumption of alcohol beverages to one drink (beer, wine or spirits) per hour.

Keep active. Don't just sit around and drink. If you stay active you tend to drink less and to be more aware of any effects alcohol may be having on you.

Beware of unfamiliar drinks. Some drinks, such as fruit drinks, can be deceiving as the alcohol content is not detectable. Therefore, it is difficult to space them properly.

Use alcohol carefully in connection with pharmaceuticals(药物). Ask your physician or pharmacist about any precautions or prohibitions and follow any advice received.

Protect others

Volunteer to be a designated driver.

Never condone or approve of excessive alcohol consumption. Intoxicated behavior is potentially dangerous and never amusing.

Don't ever let your friends drive drunk. Take their keys, have them stay the night, have them ride home with someone else, call a cab, or do whatever else is necessary, but don't let them drive!

Be a good host

Create a setting conducive to easy, comfortable socializing: soft, gentle music; low levels of noise; comfortable seating. This encourages conversation and social interaction rather than heavy drinking.

Serve food before beginning to serve drinks. This de-emphasizes the importance of alcohol and also sends the message that intoxication is not desirable.

Have a responsible bartender. If you plan to ask a friend or relative to act as bartender, make sure that person is not a drink pusher who encourages excessive consumption.

Don't have an "open bar." A responsible person needs to supervise consumption to ensure that no one drinks too much. You have both a moral and a legal responsibility to make sure that none of your guests drink too much.

Pace the drinks. Serve drinks at regular reasonable intervals. A drink-an-hour schedule is a good guide.

Push snacks. Make sure that people are eating.

Be sure to offer a diversity of attractive non-alcohol drinks.

Respect anyone's choice not to drink. Remember that about one-third of American adults choose not to drink and that a guest's reason for not drinking is the business of the guest only, not of the host. Never put anyone on the defense for not drinking.

End your gathering properly. Decide when you want the party to end and stop serving drinks well before that time. Then begin serving coffee along with substantial snacks. This provides essential non-drinking time before your guests leave.

Protect others and yourself by never driving if you think, or anyone else thinks, that you might have had too much to drink. It's always best to use a designated driver.

The good news

We can do it! While we must do even more to reduce drunk driving, we have already accomplished a great deal.

The U. S. has a low traffic fatality rate and is a very safe nation in which to drive. And it's been getting safer for decades. There is now only about one death (including the deaths of bicyclists, motorcyclists, pedestrians, auto drivers, and auto passengers) per fifty million vehicle miles traveled.

Alcohol-related traffic fatalities have dropped from 60% of all traffic deaths in 1982 down to 41% in 2002 (the most recent year for which such statistics are available).

Alcohol-related traffic fatalities per vehicle miles driven has also dropped dramatically from 1. 64 deaths per 100 million miles traveled in 1982 down to 0. 61 in 2002 (the latest year for which such statistics are available).

Alcohol-related crash fatalities have fallen 1/3 since 1982, but traffic deaths NOT associated with alcohol have jumped 43% during the same time. We're winning the battle against alcohol-related traffic fatalities, but losing the fight against traffic deaths that are not alcohol-related.

We can and must do even better

Remember: Don't ever, ever drive if you think that you may have had too much to drink. And don't let anyone else. That includes reporting drivers who may be drunk. It's always safest not to drink and drive.

> **Approximate Length: 1,158 words**
> **Suggested reading time: 8 minutes**
> **How fast do you read?** _____

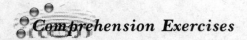

Comprehension Exercises

Complete the following exercises without referring back to the passage you have read.

1. For the sake of safety, drivers had better not drive on country roads.

2. It is ok for drivers to eat while driving.

3. If your friend has not drunk too much, you can let him drive home.

4. At a dinner party, a good atmosphere is likely to encourage people to drink.

5. Not to let your guests drink too much, it is advisable to use small cups.

6. The alcohol-related traffic death rate in the U. S. is low.

7. To fight against traffic death rate, the Americans have a long way to go.

8. Alcohol and fatigue affect drivers' _____.

9. If you want to know how much you can drink, experiment at home with your _____ or some other responsible _____.

10. Although we can take precautions, it is safest not to _____.

Words & Expressions

1. **fatality** *n.* （事故、暴力袭击中的）死亡事故

2. **intoxicated** *adv.* 喝醉的，极其兴奋的

3. **gulp** *vt.* 吞，一口吞（下）

   e.g. gulp one's food 狼吞虎咽地吃东西

4. **beverage** *n.* （正式）热或冷的饮料

5. **alcoholic** *adj.* 酒精的 non-alcoholic *adj.* 非酒精的

6. **deceive** *vt.* 欺骗

   deceive oneself 自欺欺人

7. **conducive** *adj.* 有益于

   be conducive to 有助于

   e.g. With so much noise outside, the room is hardly conducive to work. 外边这么吵，在这个房间几乎无法工作。

8. **bartender** *n.* 酒吧间销售酒精饮料的人；酒吧间男招待

9. **supervise** *vt.* 管理，指导，主管

Notes

1. Food, especially high protein food such as meat, cheese and peanuts, will help slow the absorption of alcohol into your body. 食物，尤其像肉类、奶酪、花生这样的高蛋白食物，会减慢身体对酒精的吸收。

2. Create a setting conducive to easy, comfortable socializing... 营造一种轻松、舒适的社交氛围……

3. We're winning the battle against alcohol-related traffic fatalities, but losing the fight against traffic deaths that are not alcohol-related. 我们正在赢得降低酒后驾车导致死亡的战斗，却在减少非酒后驾车导致死亡的战斗中吃败仗。

Key to the Exercises

1. Y   2. N   3. N   4. N   5. NG   6. Y   7. Y
8. reaction and judgment   9. spouse; individual   10. drink and drive

Passage 2

Directions

In this section, there is a passage with 10 blanks. You are required to select one word for each blank from a list of choices given in a word bank following the passage. Read the passage though carefully before making your choices. Each choice in the bank is identified by a letter. Please choose the corresponding letter for each item. You may not use any of the words in the bank more than once.

Our Capricious Earth

The science of climate change is easy. We burn millions of tons of __1__ fuels a year, sending millions of carbon dioxide into the atmosphere. The gas acts like the windows of a greenhouse, __2__ heat that would otherwise radiate away. Result: The world is warmer — half a degree or so in the past 100 years.

Do you think it doesn't matter? Your grandchildren will disagree. In the near term, this warming __3__ to accidental weather. More storms here; more droughts there. Over time, the __4__ consequences may include __5__ ice caps and higher sea levels. No more icebergs. No more Miami.

With 4% of the world population, the United States produces 22% of all greenhouse gas. Clearly, we __6__ some responsibility. That is why, __7__ with the threat to future Americans, the White House this week outlined a new plan to reduce greenhouse gas emissions.

The plan is __8__ modest. It delays hard limits for 10 years, hoping that tax __9__ and pollution credits will __10__ industries to act on their own. And the final goal — reduction to 1990 levels by about 2010 — is lower than many desires.

Approximate Length: 189 words

A. routinely	B. concrete	C. retaining
D. contributes	E. optional	F. disastrous
G. melted	H. bear	I. eliminate

J. painfully   K. spur   L. delivering
M. incentive   N. combined   O. fossil

1. _____   2. _____   3. _____   4. _____   5. _____
6. _____   7. _____   8. _____   9. _____   10. _____

Words & Expressions

1. **carbon dioxide** *n.* ［化］二氧化碳

2. **radiate** *vt. & vi.* 放射，辐射；传播，广播
   e.g. The heat and light radiates from the sun. 太阳向四周散发出光和热。

3. **iceberg** *n.* 冰山

4. **Miami** 迈阿密（美国地名）

5. **outline** *vt.* 提出……的纲要 *n.* 纲要，要点
   e.g. The president outlined his peace plan for the Middle East. 总统概述了他的中东和平计划。

6. **modest** *adj.* 适中的；谦逊的；腼腆的

Notes

greenhouse effect：温室效应

    是指透射阳光的密闭空间由于与外界缺乏热交换而形成的保温效应，就是太阳短波辐射可以透过大气射入地面，而地面增温后放出的长波辐射却被大气中的二氧化碳等物质所吸收，从而产生大气变暖的效应。大气中的二氧化碳就像一层厚厚的玻璃，使地球变成了一个大暖房。据估计，如果没有大气，地表平均温度就会下降到 $-23℃$，而实际地表平均温度为 $15℃$，这就是说温室效应使地表温度提高 $38℃$。

Key to the Exercises

1. O   2. C   3. D   4. F   5. G   6. H   7. N   8. J   9. M   10. K

Passage 3

Directions

The passage is followed by some questions or unfinished statement. For each of them there are four choices marked A, B, C and D. You should decide on the best choice after reading.

What Is Marriage?

Marriage socially recognized and approved union between individuals, who commit to one another with the expectation of a stable and lasting intimate relationship. It begins with a ceremony known as a wedding, which formally unites the marriage partners. A marital relationship usually involves some kind of contract, either written or specified by tradition, which defines the partners' rights and obligations to each other, to any children they may have, and to their relatives. In most contemporary industrialized societies, marriage is certified by the government.

In addition to being a personal relationship between two people, marriage is one of society's most important and basic institutions. Marriage and family serve as tools for ensuring social reproduction. Social reproduction includes providing food, clothing, and shelter for family members; raising and socializing children; and caring for the sick and elderly. In families and societies in which wealth, property, or a hereditary title is to be passed on from one generation to the next, inheritance and the production of legitimate heirs are a prime concern in marriage. However, in contemporary industrialized societies, marriage functions less as a social institution and more as a source of intimacy for the individuals involved.

Marriage is commonly defined as a partnership between two members of opposite sex known as husband and wife. However, scholars who study human culture and society disagree on whether marriage can be universally defined. The usual roles and responsibilities of the husband and wife include living together, having sexual relations only with one another, sharing economic resources, and being recognized as the parents of their children. However, unconventional forms of marriage that do not include these elements do exist. For example, scholars have studied several cultural groups in Africa and India in which husbands and wives do not live together. Instead, each spouse remains in his or her original home, and the husband is a "visitor" with sexual rights. Committed relationships between homosexuals (individuals with a sexual orientation toward people of the same sex) also challenge conventional definitions of marriage.

Debates over the definition of marriage illustrate its dual nature as both a public institution and a private, personal relationship. On the one hand, marriage involves an emotional and sexual relationship between particular human beings. At the same time, marriage is an institution that transcends the particular individuals involved in it and unites two families. In some cultures, marriage connects two families in a complicated set of property exchanges involving land, labor, and other resources. The extended family and society also share an interest in any children the couple may have. Furthermore, the legal and religious definitions of marriage and the laws that surround it usually represent the symbolic expression of core cultural norms (informal behavioral guidelines) and values.

Approximate Length: 456 words

1. Traditionally marriage _____.
   A. is merely a personal relationship between two persons
   B. involves parents' arrangement
   C. mainly functions as a social institution
   D. focuses on providing food, clothing and shelter for family members

2. Today marriage's function _____.
   A. is strengthened as a social unit
   B. is more of a source of intimacy for individuals
   C. is changing because marriage's definition is being challenged
   D. becomes more complicated

3. Scholars argue on the universal definition of marriage because _____.
   A. the function of marriage is changing with the development of society
   B. the usual roles and responsibilities of the husband and wife are changing
   C. there are some unconventional marriage forms
   D. marriage is becoming more and more personal

4. The debate over the definition of marriage reflects the fact that _____.
   A. marriage stresses individuality
   B. marriage has its dual nature
   C. marriage's traditional definition is out of date
   D. the legal definition of marriage is not accurate

5. This passage is mainly about _____.
   A. the elements of marriage
   B. the function of marriage
   C. the debate over marriage
   D. the definition of marriage

Words & Expressions

1. **commit to** 使承担义务；做出承诺，保证
   e.g We cannot commit to any concrete proposals. 我们不能允诺提供任何具体的建议。
2. **intimate** *adj.* 亲密的
   e.g. intimate friend 亲密的朋友
3. **marital** *adj.* 婚姻的
   e.g. marital status 婚姻状态
4. **obligation** *n.* 义务，责任
   e.g. take family responsibilities and obligations 承担家庭责任
5. **hereditary** *adj.* 世袭的，遗传的

6. **legitimate** *adj.* 合法的,法律上的
7. **heir** *n.* 继承人
8. **unconventional** *adj.* 非传统的
9. **dual** *adj.* 双重的
10. **transcend** *vt.* 超越,胜过
    e. g. The desire for peace transcended political differences. 对和平的渴望超越了政治上的分歧。

Notes

1. Marriage socially recognized and approved union between individuals，who commit to one another with the expectation of a stable and lasting intimate relationship. 婚姻是得到社会承认和批准的个体之间的联合,彼此做出承诺期望一种稳定和持久的亲密关系。

2. Debates over the definition of marriage illustrate its dual nature as both a public institution and a private，personal relationship. 关于对婚姻定义的辩论阐述了婚姻的双重本质即婚姻既是一种大众的制度又是一种私人、个人的关系。

3. Furthermore，the legal and religious definitions of marriage and the laws that surround it usually represent the symbolic expression of core cultural norms（informal behavioral guidelines）and values. 此外,婚姻的法律与宗教的定义与环绕婚姻的法律通常代表核心文化规范的象征表达(非正式的行为准则)和价值观。

Key to the Exercises

1. C   2. B   3. C   4. B   5. D

Passage 4

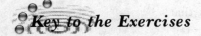 Directions

The passage is followed by some questions or unfinished statement. For each of them there are four choices marked A，B，C and D. You should decide on the best choice after reading.

A New Way of Tracing

A couple were found murdered in a parked car in a Boston suburb. The police found no clues in the car, and the case seemed doomed to the "unsolved" file. Then detectives found a witness who had seen a car pause by the murdered couple's vehicle. His description placed the car as a 1950 or 1951 Chevrolet.

Ordinarily, searching through the files for owners of elderly Chevies would have been an impossibly difficult task because there were millions of registered cars. In this case, the police had a powerful ally—the computer.

The Boston Registry of Motor Vehicles programmed its computer to screen all 1950 and 1951 Chevrolets within a fifteen-mile radius of the suburb—the area in which the police believed the murderer was most likely to be found. Within minutes, the computer uncovered one thousand of the wanted cars. A few hours of careful hand screening turned up a 1950 Chevrolet owner who lived close to the scene of the crime and who had received many traffic tickets. He was among the first suspects to be investigated, and evidence linking him to the murdered couple was found. He was taken into custody and given his share of punishment.

This culprit is just one of a steadily growing number of lawbreakers captured by computers, which many police consider the most important crime-busting device inaugurated since the patrol car and police radio, department computers are doing everything from identifying crooks by analyzing their working habits and fingerprints to forecasting crime hot spots. Evidence of the computer's extraordinary police abilities is steadily piling up. In 1961, Chicago inaugurated its police computer center as part of an overall police department streamlining. By 1965, computers were playing a part in 95 percent of all the city's police operations. That year, while the national crime rate spiraled up 13 percent, the average crime rate in Chicago dropped 12 percent, and major crimes went down 17 percent.

One of the most important ways in which computers are helping to control crime is by breaking a traditional law enforcement roadblocking—identification. Take fingerprints, for example.

Not long ago, a burglar looted a New York store. As part of his nightly cleanup procedure, the manager had wiped off the glass counter top. Detectives dispatched to the scene, found it smudged with fresh prints, only one of which was sharp. It was the kind of case which once would have gone unsolved because it would take a small army of clerks years to thumb through the files looking for a print that matched up. But with computers, this was no longer a problem.

Approximate Length: 435 words

1. The passage is mainly about _____.
   A. the crime patterns in Chicago   B. the increase of crimes in Chicago
   C. how police investigated the murder   D. the role computers play in fighting crimes
2. Catching the suspect of the murder was made possible by _____.
   A. identifying his car by a witness

    B. asking a witness to describe him

    C. identifying his car with the help of the computer

    D. his many traffic tickets

3. The word "culprit" (Line 1, Para. 4) probably means _____.

    A. criminal   B. crime   C. theft   D. murder

4. As a result of introducing computers to police operations, _____.

    A. the national crime rate increased

    B. Chicago's crime rate remained at its previous level

    C. major crimes dropped though average crimes increased

    D. crimes decreased in Chicago

5. Which of the following is NOT true?

    A. Computers help police predict where crime may increase.

    B. Computers help police find the murderer in his car.

    C. Police department computers help solve crimes.

    D. Computers are a lot of help in identifying fingerprints.

Words & Expressions

1. **doom to** 注定,命定

    e. g. Their plan was doomed to fail from the start. 他们的计划从一开始就注定要失败。

2. **ally** *n.* 同盟国,支持者

3. **radius** *n.* 半径,范围,界限

4. **thumb through** 翻查

5. **cleanup** *n.* 扫除,清扫

6. **dispatch** *vt.* 分派,派遣

    e. g. dispatch letters 发送信件

Notes

1. Ordinarily, searching through the files for owners of elderly Chevies would have been an impossibly difficult task because there were millions of registered cars. 通常,在过去对老式雪佛莱车主档案的调查是一件不可能的任务,因为有成百万已登记的汽车。

2. Evidence of the computer's extraordinary police abilities is steadily piling up. 计算机特别的监控能力正在逐渐上升。

3. As part of his nightly cleanup procedure, the manager had wiped off the glass counter top. 作为他每晚清理过程的一部分,这个经理总是打扫这个玻璃柜台面。

Key to the Exercises

1. D   2. C   3. A   4. D   5. B

Passage 1

Directions

There are 10 questions after the passage. Go over the passage quickly and answer the questions in the given time.

For questions 1 – 7, mark

Y (for YES)   if the statement agrees with the information given in the passage;

N (for NO)   if the statement contradicts the information given in the passage;

NG (for NOT GIVEN) if the information is not given in the passage.

For questions 8 – 10, complete the sentences with the information given in the passage.

Water Shortage

Picture a "ghost ship" sinking into the sand, left to rot on dry land by a receding sea. Then imagine dust storms sweeping up toxic pesticides and chemical fertilizers from the dry seabed and spewing (呕吐)them across towns and villages.

Seem like a scene from a movie about the end of the world? For people living near the Aral sea（咸海）in Central Asia, it's all too real. Thirty years ago, government planners diverted the rivers that flow into the sea in order to irrigate (provide water for) farmland. As a result, the sea has shrunk to half its original size, stranding（使搁浅）ships on dry land. The seawater has tripled in salt content and become polluted, killing all 24 native species of fish.

Similar large-scale efforts to redirect water in other parts of the world have also ended in ecological crisis, according to numerous environmental groups. But many countries continue to build massive dams and irrigation systems, even though such projects can create more problems than they fix. Why? People in many parts of the world are desperate for water, and more people will need more water in the next century.

"Growing populations will worsen problems with water," says Peter H. Gleick, an environmental scientist at the Pacific Institute for studies in Development, Environment, and Security, a research organization in California. He fears that by the year 2025, as many as one-third of the world's projected (预测的) 8.3 billion people will suffer from water shortages.

Where water goes

Only 2.5 percent of all water on Earth is freshwater, water suitable for drinking and growing food, says Sandra Postel, director of the Global Water Policy Project in Amherst, Mass. Two-thirds of this freshwater is locked in glaciers and ice caps (冰盖). In fact, only a tiny percentage of freshwater is part of the water cycle, in which water evaporates and rises into the atmosphere, then condenses and falls back to Earth as precipitation (rain or snow).

Some precipitation runs off land to lakes and oceans, and some becomes groundwater, water that seeps into the earth. Much of this renewable freshwater ends up in remote places like the Amazon river basin in Brazil, where few people live. In fact, the world's population has access to only 12,500 cubic kilometers of freshwater—about the amount of water in Lake Superior (苏必利尔湖). And people use half of this amount already. "If water demand continues to climb rapidly," says Postel, "there will be severe shortages and damage to the aquatic (水的) environment."

Close to home

Water woes (灾难) may seem remote to people living in rich countries like the United States. But Americans could face serious water shortages too, especially in areas that rely on groundwater. Groundwater accumulates in aquifers (地下蓄水层), layers of sand and gravel that lie between soil and bedrock. (For every liter of surface water, more than 90 liters are hidden underground). Although the United States has large aquifers, farmers, ranchers, and cities are tapping many of them for water faster than nature can replenish (补充) it. In northwest Texas, for example, overpumping has shrunk groundwater supplies by 25 percent, according to Postel.

Americans may face even more urgent problems from pollution. Drinking water in the United States is generally safe and meets high standards. Nevertheless, one in five Americans every day unknowingly drinks tap water contaminated with bacteria and chemical wastes, according to the Environmental Protection Agency. In Milwaukee, 400,000 people fell ill in 1993 after drinking tap water tainted with cryptosporidium (隐孢子虫), a microbe (微生物) that causes fever, diarrhea (腹泻) and vomiting.

The source

Where do contaminants come from? In developing countries, people dump raw (未经处理的) sewage (污水) into the same streams and rivers from which they draw water for drinking and cooking; about 250 million people a year get sick from water borne (饮水传染的) diseases.

In developed countries, manufacturers use 100,000 chemical compounds to make a wide range of products. Toxic chemicals pollute water when released untreated into rivers and lakes. (Certain compounds, such as polychlorinated biphenyls (多氯化联二苯), or PCBs, have been banned in the United States.)

But almost everyone contributes to water pollution. People often pour household cleaners, car antifreeze, and paint thinners (稀释剂) down the drain; all of these contain hazardous chemicals. Scientists studying water in the San Francisco Bay reported in 1996 that 70 percent of the pollutants could be traced to household waste.

Farmers have been criticized for overusing herbicides and pesticides, chemicals that kill weeds and insects pollute water as well. Farmers also use nitrates, nitrogen-rich fertilizer that helps plants grow but that can wreak havoc (大破坏) on the environment. Nitrates are swept away by surface runoff to lakes and seas. Too many nitrates "over-enrich" these bodies of water, encouraging the buildup of algae, or microscopic plants that live on the surface of the water. Algae deprive the water of oxygen that fish need to survive, at times choking off life in an entire body of water.

What's the solution

Water expert Gleick advocates conservation and local solutions to water-related problems; governments, for instance, would be better off building small-scale dams rather than huge and disruptive projects like the one that ruined the Aral Sea.

"More than 1 billion people worldwide don't have access to basic clean drinking water," says Gleick. "There has to be a strong push on the part of everyone-governments and ordinary people to make sure we have a resource so fundamental to life."

> Approximate Length: 1,000 words
> Suggested reading time: 7 minutes
> How fast do you read? _____

Comprehension Exercises

Complete the following exercises without referring back to the passage you have read.

1. That the huge water projects have diverted the rivers causes the Aral Sea to shrink.

2. The construction of massive dams and irrigation projects does more good than harm.

3. The chief causes of water shortage are population growth and water pollution.

4. The problems Americans face concerning water are groundwater shrinkage and tap water pollution.

5. According to the passage, all water pollutants come from household waste.

6. The people living in the United States will not be faced with water shortages.

7. Water expert Gleick has come up with the best solution to water-related problems.

8. According to Peter H. Gleick, by the year 2025, as many as _____ of the world's people will suffer from water shortages.

9. Two-thirds of the freshwater on Earth is locked in _____.

10. In developed countries, before toxic chemicals are released into rivers and lakes, they should be treated in order to avoid _____.

Words & Expressions

1. **recede** *vi.* (水)退,退去;(景物、声音)逐渐远去直至消失

   e.g. Flood waters finally began to recede in November. 洪水终于在11月间开始消退。

2. **divert** *vt.* 改变方向

   e.g. divert attention 转变注意力

3. **content** *n.* 内容,此处意为海水的含盐量

4. **ecological** *adj.* 生态的

   e.g. ecological system 生态系统

5. **evaporate** *vt.* (使)蒸发;(使液体)挥发;(感觉)逐渐消失

   e.g. Hopes of reaching an agreement are becoming to evaporate. 达成协议的希望开始逝去。

6. **condense** *vi. & vt.* 浓缩,凝缩

7. **have access to** 有机会接触;有权利接触

   e.g. Students have access to the school library. 学生有权借用图书馆的图书。

8. **contaminate** *vt.* 污染,弄脏

   contaminant *n.* 污染物,污染源

9. **drain** *n.* 下水道,排水装置

10. **microscopic** *adj.* 显微镜的,极微小的

    microscope *n.* 显微镜

11. **disruptive** *adj.* 造成分裂的

Notes

1. Similar large-scale efforts to redirect water in other parts of the world have also ended in ecological crisis, according to numerous environmental groups. 据大量的环境保护组织的调查,在世界其他地方,大规模的类似努力(即指巨大河流改道水利工程)也以导致生态危机而告终。

end in 以……而告终

2. But many countries continue to build massive dams and irrigation systems, even though such projects can create more problems than they fix. 虽然大量的水坝和灌溉系统的建造带来的问题多于其所能解决的问题,很多国家仍在继续这样做。

3. "If water demand continues to climb rapidly," says Postel, "there will be severe shortages and damage to the aquatic（水的）environment." Postel 说:"如果水的需求量快速攀升,将会出现严重的水荒并对水环境造成破坏。"

4. Although the United States has large aquifers, farmers, ranchers, and cities are tapping many of them for water faster than nature can replenish it. 虽然美国有大量的地下蓄水层、农夫和农场管理人员,但城市消耗这些资源的速度要大于自然所能补给的速度。

5. Nevertheless, one in five Americans every day unknowingly drinks tap water contaminated with bacteria and chemical wastes, according to the Environmental Protection Agency. 然而,根据环境保护机构的报告,每天每五位美国人中就有一位在不知情的情况下饮用细菌和化学废料污染过的自来水。

Key to the Exercises

1. Y   2. N   3. Y   4. Y   5. N   6. N   7. NG

8. one-third   9. glaciers and ice caps   10. water pollution

Passage 2

Directions

In this section, there is a passage with 10 blanks. You are required to select one word for each blank from a list of choices given in a word bank following the passage. Read the passage through carefully before making your choices. Each choice in the bank is identified by a letter. Please choose the corresponding letter for each item. You may not use any of the words in the bank more than once.

The Warming Earth

There's no question that the Earth is getting hotter. The real questions are: How much of the warming is our fault, and are we ___1___ to slow the devastation by controlling our insatiable ___2___ for fossil fuels?

Global warming can seem too ___3___ to worry about, or too uncertain—something projected by the same computer ___4___ that often can't get next week's weather right. On a raw（湿冷的）winter day you might think that a few degrees of warming wouldn't be such a bad thing anyway. And no doubt about it：Warnings about ___5___ change can sound like an environmentalist's scare tactic, meant to force us out of our cars and restrict our lifestyles.

Comforting thoughts, perhaps. Unfortunately, however, the Earth has some discomforting news. From Alaska to the snowy peaks of the Andes the world is heating up right now, and fast. Globally, the ___6___ is up 1°F over the past century, but some of the coldest, most remote spots have warmed much more. The results aren't pretty. Ice is ___7___, rivers are running dry, and coasts are ___8___, threatening communities.

The ___9___ are happening largely out of sight. But they shouldn't be out of mind, because they are omens of what's in store for the ___10___ of the planet.

> **Approximate Length：208 words**

A. remote   B. techniques   C. consisting
D. rest   E. willing   F. climate
G. skill   H. appetite   I. melting
J. vanishing   K. eroding   L. temperature
M. curiosity   N. changes   O. skillful

1. _____   2. _____   3. _____   4. _____   5. _____
6. _____   7. _____   8. _____   9. _____   10. _____

Words & Expressions

1. **devastation** *n.* 毁坏,破坏
2. **insatiable** *adj.* 不能满足的,极贪心的
3. **tactic** *n.* 战术,达成目标的方法
4. **omen** *n.* 征兆,预兆

Notes

1. ... slow the devastation by controlling our insatiable appetite for fossil fuels.... 通过控制我们无止境地获取化石燃料的欲望来减缓气温升高的速度。

   appetite for... 对……的欲望,渴望

2. Global warming can seem too remote to worry about. 全球气候变暖似乎离我们太遥远,以至于

我们无须为此担心。

　　此句用了 too...to... 句型。

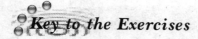

Key to the Exercises

1. E   2. H   3. A   4. B   5. F   6. L   7. I   8. K   9. N   10. D

Passage 3

> **Directions**
>
> The passage is followed by some questions or unfinished statements. For each of them there are four choices marked A, B, C and D. You should decide on the best choice after reading.

The New Generation in Japan

　　Managers in Japan used to be shocked by the strange young employees they called new mankind. A new mankind is more direct than the traditional Japanese. He acts almost like a westerner. He does not live for the company, and will move on if he gets the offer of a better job. He is not keen on overtime, especially if he has a date with a girl. He has his own plans for his free time, and they may not include drinking or playing golf with the boss. All pretty wild staff a few years back, but these days managers accept that the life of a new mankind has much to offer.

　　A survey shows that only a few business managers are in favor of some traditional practices associated with job security and a guaranteed level of pay. These practices include long hours and transferring employees to new posts where they may be separated from their families. The vast majority of business managers think that efforts should be made to reduce working hours, and that personal freedom should be respected.

　　Japan is embarrassed by the international attention given to Japanese working conditions. In 1987 it reduced the number of hours that may be legally worded （计数，计时） from 48 per week to 46. Eventually Japan hopes for a 40-hour working week. But enforcement of the law is not so effective. The Labor Ministry wants to get the support of employees for a wide-range plan that includes a five-day working week, paid holidays would be lowered to 1,800 hours a year by 1992. Japanese workers at present work more than 2,000 hours a year, and no more than 40%, mainly in big firms, have Saturdays off.

Approximate Length：290 words

1. The young employees are more _____.
   A. roundabout   B. direct   C. simple   D. worldly
2. According to the passage, a new mankind lives for his _____.
   A. country   B. company   C. boss   D. family and himself
3. The traditional practices include _____.
   A. job security   B. guaranteed level of pay
   C. long working hours   D. all of the above
4. The majority of Japanese business managers like _____.
   A. reduced working hours   B. more personal freedom
   C. more job transfers   D. both A and B
5. At present Japanese workers work more than _____.
   A. 1,800 hours a year   B. 1,992 hours a year
   C. 2,000 hours a year   D. none of the above

Words & Expressions

1. **be in favor of** 支持，赞同
   e.g. We are in favor of her promotion to president. 我们赞成她升为总裁。
2. **guarantee** *vt.* 保证，担保
   e.g. Many shopkeepers guarantee satisfaction to customers. 许多店主对顾客许诺定让他们满意。
3. **embarrass** *vt.* 使困窘，使局促不安；阻碍，麻烦
   e.g. He was embarrassed by debts. 他因债务而局促不安。
4. **enforcement** *n.* 执行，强制
   e.g. budget enforcement 预算执行

Notes

1. All pretty wild staff a few years back, but these days managers accept that the life of a new mankind has much to offer. 过去几年经理们认为新新人类的生活充满了疯狂，而如今他们认同这种生活也是有许多可以借鉴的地方。
2. A survey shows that only a few business managers are in favor of some traditional practices associated with job security and a guaranteed level of pay. 一项调查显示只有少部分经理赞同与工作保障以及薪水保障相联系的传统操作方法。

3. Japan is embarrassed by the international attention given to Japanese working conditions.
日本因其工作制度引起了国际关注而局促不安。

Key to the Exercises

1. B   2. D   3. D   4. D   5. C

Passage 4

Directions

The passage is followed by some questions or unfinished statements. For each of them there are four choices marked A, B, C and D. You should decide on the best choice after reading.

Population Explosion

A very important world problem—in fact, I am inclined to say it is the most important of all the great world problems which face us at present time—is the rapidly increasing pressure of population on land and on land resources.

It is not so much the actual population of the world but its rate of increase, which is the most important. It works out to be about 1.6 percent net annual increase. In terms of numbers this means something like 40 to 55 million additional people every year. Canada has population of 20 million, rather less than 6 months' climb in world population. And there are 10 million people in Australia. So, it takes the world less than three months to add to itself a population, which peoples that vast country. Let us come to our own crowded country—England and Wales: 45-50 million people—just about a year's supply. By this time tomorrow, and every day, there will be added to the earth about 120,000 extra people—just about the population of the city of New York.

I am not talking about birthrate. This is net increase. To give you some idea of birthrate, look at the second hand of your watch. Every second three babies are born somewhere in the world. Another baby! Another baby! Another baby! You cannot speak quickly enough to keep pace with the birthrate.

This enormous increase of population will create immense problems. By 2000 A. D. , unless something desperate happens, there will be as many as 7,000,000,000 people on the surface of this earth! So this is a problem which you are going to see in your lifetime.

Approximate Length: 275 words

1. The topic for the passage is _____.
   A. The Lack of Land Resources
   B. Population Explosion
   C. Your Lifetime
   D. The Birthrate

2. According to the author, _____ is the most important for population pressure.
   A. the enormous amount of world population
   B. the birthrate
   C. the net increase rate
   D. the population explosion in Australia

3. It can be learned from paragraph 2 that _____.
   A. in less than 6 months, to the world population 20 million will be added
   B. three months later, to the population in the world 10 million will be added
   C. in less than three months, to the world population 10 million will be added
   D. one year later, the population of England and Wales will double

4. Which of the following is TRUE?
   A. After 24 hours, 120 thousand babies were born.
   B. The birthrate is 180 babies every minute.
   C. During a year, about 45 million people are born.
   D. After a day, York will have 120,000 extra people.

5. "… something desperate happens" in the last paragraph can be best replaced by _____.
   A. the world wars break out
   B. people are in despair
   C. birth control policy is adopted
   D. people realize the seriousness of the population problem

Words & Expressions

1. **be inclined to do sth.** 倾向于做某事
   e. g. I am inclined to be ill after eating fish. 我吃完鱼后就想吐。

2. **people** *vt.* 供以人民，使人民居住
   e. g. a thickly peopled district 人口稠密的地区

3. **net** *adj.* 净得的
   e. g. net profit 纯利；net weight 净重

4. **keep pace with** 并驾齐驱

e. g. keep pace with the development of electronics 跟上电子学的发展

5. **immense** *adj.* 极广大的，无边的，[口]非常好的

 e. g. The government will be building new hotels, an immense stadium, and a fine new swimming pool. 政府打算建造许多新的旅馆，一个巨大的露天运动场和一个漂亮的新游泳池。

6. **desperate** *adj.* 不顾一切的，拼死的，令人绝望的

 e. g. a desperate cry for help 绝望的呼救声

Notes

1. It is not so much the actual population of the world but its rate of increase, which is the most important. 最重要的问题并不是实际的世界人口数量，而是世界人口的增长比率。

2. To give you some idea of birthrate, look at the second hand of your watch. 为了能够使你对出生率有一定的了解，看一眼你的手表的秒针吧。

3. By 2000 A. D. , unless something desperate happens, there will be as many as 7,000,000,000 people on the surface of this earth! 到公元 2000 年，除非世界末日到来，否则地球表面的人口将达到 70 亿之多。

Key to the Exercises

1. B   2. C   3. C   4. B   5. A

Unit 6

Passage 1

Directions

There are 10 questions after the passage. Go over the passage quickly and answer the questions in the given time.

For questions 1 – 7, mark

Y (for YES)   if the statement agrees with the information given in the passage;

N (for NO)   if the statement contradicts the information given in the passage;

NG (for NOT GIVEN) if the information is not given in the passage.

For questions 8 – 10, complete the sentences with the information given in the passage.

A World without Children

We shouldn't worry about overpopulation, argues Mark Leonard. The real problem is quite different. When global population has reached beyond six billion, there has come the chance for UN officials to warn of the dangers of more and more people sharing fewer and fewer resources.

At first glance the figures seem frightening. It took all of time for world population to reach one billion in 1804. Then 123 years for it to grow to two billion in 1927 and 33 years to reach three billion in 1960. Fourteen years later, in 1974, it had reached four billion; by 1987 we were five billion and the latest billion were born in the past few years.

However, maybe we should use the occasion to bury Malthusian predictions. Thomas Malthus (马尔萨斯,英国经济学家) was the economist who, in 1799, said that the human race would soon die of starvation. Populations, he argued, grow exponentially—2,4,8,16,32—while the availability of resources grows only arithmetically—2,4,6,8,10. Result: the world must run out of food and starve. In fact, for most of the globe, successive generations since Malthus have been better nourished. But the reason to bury rather than praise Malthus is not because of his unwarranted pessimism but because his analysis is diametrically wrong. It is not overpopulation that is most likely to kill off humanity, but underpopulation.

Population growth declines in developed countries

While India and China will continue to grow in the medium term, the developed world is shrinking before our eyes. The Japanese government has predicted that its population will have fallen from 126 million today to just 500 by the end of 21st century and to a single person in AD 3500. However absurd that may be, it is at least a scare in the right direction. Britain is just one of 61 countries where insufficient babies are being born to replace the population. For a population to remain stable, women must have an average of 2.1 babies each. In the UK, women are having just 1.7. In Japan it is 1.4.

In Spain it is just 1.15 (in some parts of Spain it has dropped below one). The unexpectedly sharp decline in fertility (生育) around the world has forced all forecasters including the UN to revise their predictions of when world population will peak before falling back. The UN's best guess is nine billion by 2050, but it admits the total could peak at 7.5 billion by 2040. But whether in 2040 or 2050, fall back it certainly will. The increasing status of women around the world is to blame. Malthus' generation never considered the possibility that women would go to work or choose the size of their families.

Problems and impacts caused by depopulation

In advanced industrial societies such as Britain, a smaller population would mean an end to soaring property prices, unemployment and homelessness. The building trade would disappear, and green belts would be safe. Public transport systems would suffer from overcapacity, rather than overcrowding. Class sizes would shrink and schools would have to merge or close, or reinvent themselves as lifelong learning centers.

Other impacts include the continuing disappearance of extended families. People will be lonelier and more dependent on institutionalized long-term care. Someone will have to pay for this, as the pension organizations have warned. On the plus side, fewer polluters may mean an end to global warming, while acid rain, poisoned seas and rivers would become things of the past.

But a shrinking population also brings new problems. At a time when developed countries are once again relying on labor, as economies move from production to knowledge or service industries, their workforces will decrease severely. By the end of this year the population of working age in Germany, Italy and Japan will have started to decline by 1 percent annually. Initially this will end unemployment but then it will create chronic labor shortages. Businesses will enter permanent recession as demand collapses due to an ever-contracting consumer base.

The depopulation of the north and the misbalanced age structures of both north and south will change the balance of global power. For Britain, this means totally reassessing its value system. At the Labor Party conference Tony Blair said: "In the 18th century land was our resource. In the 19th and 20th century, it was plant and capital. Today it is people." He meant that in a knowledge-based economy Britain must invest in its citizens' education if it is to prosper. The problem may be having enough citizens to educate.

Measures to solve problems

Sweden is one country that has seen the warning signs and is introducing taxation policies to make parenting more attractive. The idea of a dowry (资助) for young families is another way to bribe people into parenthood. A government that is serious about population must also try to rebalance work and family life, and look beyond the usual panacea (灵丹妙药) of parental leave.

One key to economic and social success will be reevaluation of the immigration system. Ownership of the best land or natural resources will become less important than who has the best population, and European countries may find that "managing borders" will be crucial to their success. Instead of trying desperately to keep people from the developing world out, the west will have to encourage imagination. Countries such as Ireland and Canada have already shown the way in attracting the rich and the skilled from around the world with tax breaks.

The most powerful means of attracting good-quality imaginations would be to create a country that was worth living in. Just as the Statue of Liberty inspired and attracted generations of the brightest and most entrepreneurial (企业的) immigrants to the U.S. in the 19th and 20th centuries, it is the countries that offer an attractive way of life that will thrive in the 21st. Here Britain is peculiarly well placed. Not only does it have an amazing infrastructure for cultural diplomacy (the British Council, BBC World Service and so on), but it already stands for creativity and openness to the world.

Finally, and most ominously, there are implications for personal taxation. Just as countries have reduced their rates of corporation tax over the past few years to attract inward investment, we might see countries cutting income tax to attract skilled workers. The implications for welfare states and public services could be very damaging.

The developed world's immigration policies have always been based on its own need, and the developing world already suffers from a brain and skills drain because of the policies in the industrialized world. In a world where we make up only a tiny percentage of the population and where our continued prosperity and security depends on making deals with others—from nuclear security to free trade—it will not be in our interests to be hypocritical or selfish about immigration.

We need a sensible global policy that replaces our fears about there being too many people and concentrates on whether we have the skills to compete. We have to stop fussing about single mothers and immigration, and recognize that in an interdependent world it is in all our interests to give the new born of human race a world worth living in.

> Approximate Length: 1,194 words
> Suggested reading time: 9 minutes
> How fast do you read? _____

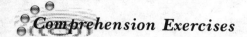

Comprehension Exercises

Complete the following exercises without referring back to the passage you have read.

1. This passage is mainly about the likely impacts of depopulation in developed countries and the countermeasures.

2. Malthusian predictions about world population still hold true even today.

3. Women's improved status is responsible for the decline of world population.

4. The world's environment will be improved as a result of general population decline.

5. On the whole, the world will receive more positive effects than negative ones from a smaller population.

6. Many problems have arisen in the developed countries as a result of depopulation.

7. It is predicted that western countries will not encourage immigration because of underpopulation.

8. The Swedish government encourages child birth by _____.

9. Countries that hope to attract good-quality imaginations must _____.

10. The developed world's immigration policies have resulted in the developing countries' loss of _____.

Words & Expressions

1. **starvation** *n.* 饥饿,饿死
   starve *vi.* (使)饿,(使)饿死
   e.g. starve to death 饿死

2. **successive** *adj.* 继续的,连续的
   e.g. successive victories 连胜

3. **warrant** *vt.* 证明……为正常;有理由,有权利;保证 *n.* (做某事的)充分理由
   unwarranted *adj.* 无正当理由的
   e.g. This tiny crowd does not warrant such a large police presence. 没有理由出动这么多警察来对付这一小群人。

4. **absurd** *adj.* 荒谬的,可笑的,愚蠢的

e. g. It is absurd to do sth. 做……很荒唐

5. **merge** *vi.* merge in/into/with... (使)合并,融合

e. g. Roger is to merge with BMW, the German car manufacturer. 罗弗公司要和德国汽车制造商宝马公司合并。

6. **on the plus side** 从正面来说

on the positive side 从积极的角度来看

7. **reassess** *vt.* 重新评价,重新评估

assess *vt.* 评价

assessment *n.* 评价

8. **diplomacy** *n.* 外交;外交手段

9. **drain** *vt.* (指液体)(使)流出,排出,(使)干涸

e. g. Deep ditches were dug to drain the fields. 挖了深沟以排干田里的水。

Notes

1. But the reason to bury rather than praise Malthus is not because of his unwarranted pessimism but because his analysis is diametrically wrong. 我们之所以摒弃而非支持马尔萨斯的理论,不是因为它的毫无根据的悲观论调,而是因为它是完全错误的。

2. Public transport systems would suffer from overcapacity, rather than overcrowding. 公共交通系统的损失是因为其容量过大而不是因为过分拥挤造成的。

3. Businesses will enter permanent recession as demand collapses due to an ever-contracting consumer base. 由于消费群体的日益减小导致需求量的下降,企业将进入持久的衰退期。

4. Not only does it have an amazing infrastructure for cultural diplomacy (the British Council, BBC World Service and so on), but it already stands for creativity and openness to the world. 它(指英国)不仅有着令人惊羡的文化外交(如英国议会,BBC 国际服务公司等),而且它也代表着创造性和开放性。

　　这是一个由 not only... but (also) 引导的倒装句。

5. In a world where we make up only a tiny percentage of the population and where our continued prosperity and security depends on making deals with others—from nuclear security to free trade—it will not be in our interests to be hypocritical or selfish about immigration. 我们(指发达国家)的人口只占世界人口的很少一部分,我们持续的繁荣和安定取决于如何和外界打交道——包括核安全和自由贸易在内,在这样的条件下,采取自私的或吹毛求疵的移民政策将对我们不利。

　　这个句子中,两个 where 引导了两个定语从句修饰短语 In a world,主句是 it will not be in our interests to be hypocritical or selfish about immigration.

Key to the Exercises

1. Y　　2. N　　3. Y　　4. Y　　5. NG　　6. Y　　7. N

8. introducing taxation policies　9. create a country worth living in　10. brain and skills

Passage 2

Directions

In this section, there is a passage with 10 blanks. You are required to select one word for each blank from a list of choices given in a word bank following the passage. Read the passage through carefully before making your choices. Each choice in the bank is identified by a letter. Please choose the corresponding letter for each item. You may not use any of the words in the bank more than once.

Personal Relationship

The concept of friendship takes different forms in a variety of cultures. In America, you may make different friends when you have different activities. You would not be expected to introduce these friends to one another. Americans, especially people in ___1___ areas, move often in their lifetime, so friendships tend to change many times.

In America, unmarried people of the opposite sex freely ___2___ with each other. They can also date many people at the same time. If they go steady, certain restraints would be expected. It would be ___3___ to date anyone else.

Married couples may have friends of the opposite sex, but there are some restraints on such ___4___ friendships. They are not expected to go to activities that would be considered ___5___, such as going to a movie or having a private dinner together. Most married couples expect their partners to be ___6___.

Americans may seem ___7___ on first encounter, so it may be necessary for others to ___8___ a relationship. They may also feel intimidated by a foreigner since they think they have nothing in common. Generally speaking, Americans are ___9___ to developing friendships with foreigners, but you have to make "the first ___10___".

There are no fixed rules which govern friendships in America. As you spend more time within the culture, you will gain a greater understanding of what is appropriate.

Approximate Length: 231 words

A. associate   B. acquired   C. move

D. improper   E. receptive   F. consistent

G. distant   H. initiate   I. urban

J. prominent   K. outside   L. countless

M. romantic   N. breakdown   O. faithful

1. _____   2. _____   3. _____   4. _____   5. _____

6. _____   7. _____   8. _____   9. _____   10. _____

Words & Expressions

1. **date** *vt.* 约会

   e.g. date sb. 与某人约会

2. **restraint** *n.* 克制,阻止,约束

   e.g. without restraint 自由地;无拘无束地;放纵地

3. **encounter** *vt.* 遭遇(危险,困难等);遭逢(敌人);邂逅(友人) *n.* 遭遇(尤指敌人)

   e.g. on first encounter 初次相遇

4. **intimidate** *vt.* 胁迫,威迫

   e.g. intimidate sb. into doing sth. 胁迫某人做某事

5. **have nothing in common** (与某人)没有共同语言

   have little in common (与某人)共同语言很少

   have much in common (与某人)共同语言很多

Notes

1. Generally speaking, Americans are receptive to developing friendships with foreigners, but you have to make "the first move". 一般来说,美国人乐于同外国人发展友谊,但你必须首先采取"主动措施"。

2. There are no fixed rules which govern friendships in America. 在美国,就建立和维持友谊而言,没有固定的规则。

Key to the Exercises

1. I   2. A   3. D   4. K   5. M   6. O   7. G   8. H   9. E   10. C

Passage 3

The passage is followed by some questions or unfinished statements. For each of

them there are four choices marked A , B , C and D . You should decide on the best
choice after reading .

What Is Teaching and What Is Learning?

So long as teachers fail to distinguish between teaching and learning , they will continue to undertake to do for children that which only children can do for themselves . Teaching children to read is not passing reading on to them . It is certainly not endless hours spent in activities about reading . Douglas insists that "reading cannot be taught directly and schools should stop trying to do the impossible . "

Teaching and learning are two entirely different processes . They differ in kind and function . The function of teaching is to create the conditions and the climate that will make it possible for children to devise the most efficient system for teaching themselves to read . Teaching is also public activity . It can be seen and observed .

Learning to read involves all that each individual does not make sense of the world of printed language . Almost all of it is private , for learning is an occupation of the mind , and that process is not open to public scrutiny .

If teacher and learner roles are not interchangeable , what then can be done through teaching that will aid the child in the quest for knowledge? Smith has one principal rule for all teaching instructions . "Make learning to read easily , which means making reading a meaningful , enjoyable and frequent experience for children . "

When the roles of teacher and learner are seen for what they are , and when both teacher and learner fulfill them appropriately , then much of the pressure and feeling of failure for both is eliminated . Learning to read is made easier when teachers create an environment where children are given the opportunity to solve the problem of learning to read by reading .

Approximate Length: 277 words

1. The problem with the reading course as mentioned in the first paragraph is that
   _____ .

   A. it is one of the most difficult school courses

   B. students spend endless hours in reading

   C. reading tasks are assigned with little guidance

   D. too much time is spent in teaching of reading

2. The teaching of reading will be successful if _____ .

A. teachers can improve conditions at school for the students

B. teachers can enable students to develop their own way of reading

C. teachers can devise the most efficient system for reading

D. teachers can make their teaching activities observably

3. The word "scrutiny"(Para. 3)most probably means _____.

   A. inquiry   B. observation   C. control   D. suspicion

4. According to the passage, learning to read will no longer be a difficult task when _____.

A. children become highly motivated

B. teacher and learner roles are interchangeable

C. teaching helps children in the search for knowledge

D. reading enriches children's experience

5. The main idea of the passage is that _____.

A. teachers should do as little as possible in helping students learn to read

B. teachers should encourage students to read as widely as possible

C. reading ability is something acquired rather than taught

D. reading is more complicated than generally believed

Words & Expressions

1. **undertake** *vt.* 承担，担任

   e. g. The lawyer undertook the case without a fee. 这律师免费承办那个案件。

2. **make sense of** 了解……的意义，懂得

   e. g. Can you make sense of what he says? 你理解他的话吗？

3. **eliminate** *vt.* 排除，消除

   e. g. She has been eliminated from the swimming race because she did not win any of the practice races. 她已被取消了游泳比赛，因为她在训练赛中没有取得名次。

Notes

1. So long as teachers fail to distinguish between teaching and learning，they will continue to undertake to do for children that which only children can do for themselves. 如果教师不能将教与学区分开来，他们将继续为孩子们承担那些只有孩子自己才能完成的事情。

2. The function of teaching is to create the conditions and the climate that will make it possible for children to devise the most efficient system for teaching themselves to read. 教学的功能就在于要营造种种环境和氛围使孩子们有可能找出教会自己阅读的最有效的方法。

3. Learning to read involves all that each individual does not make sense of the world of printed language. 学习阅读涉及及读懂每个人还没有了解的书本世界的全部。

4. If teacher and learner roles are not interchangeable, what then can be done through

teaching that will aid the child in the quest for knowledge? 如果教师和学习者的角色是不可互换的，那么在帮助孩子寻求知识的教学过程中又能做些什么呢？

5. Learning to read is made easier when teachers create an environment where children are given the opportunity to solve the problem of learning to read by reading. 当教师营造一种使孩子们有机会通过阅读来解决学会阅读这一问题的环境时，学会如何阅读就会变得简单起来。

Key to the Exercises

1. D   2. B   3. B   4. A   5. C

Passage 4

Directions

The passage is followed by some questions or unfinished statements. For each of them there are four choices marked A, B, C and D. You should decide on the best choice after reading.

The Value of Scarce Material

Resources can be said to be scarce in both an absolute and relative sense: the surface of the Earth is finite, imposing absolute scarcity; but the scarcity that concerns economists is the relative scarcity of resources in different uses. Materials used for one purpose cannot at the same time be used for other purposes; if the quantity of an input is limited, the increased use of it in one manufacturing process must cause it to become less available for other uses.

The cost of a product in terms of money may not measure its true cost to society. The true cost of, say, the construction of a supersonic jet is the value of the schools and refrigerators that will never be built as a result. Every act of production uses up some of society's available resources; it means the foregoing of an opportunity to produce something else. In deciding how to use resources most effectively to satisfy the wants of the community, this opportunity cost must ultimately be taken into account.

In a market economy the price of goods and the quantity supplied depend on the cost of making it, and that cost, ultimately, is the cost of not making other goods. The market mechanism enforces this relationship. The cost of, say, a pair of shoes is the price of the leather, the labor, the fuel, and other elements used up in producing them. But the price of these inputs, in turn, depends on what they can produce elsewhere—if the leather can be used to produce handbags that are valued highly by consumers, the prices of leather will be bid up correspondingly.

Approximate Length：273 words

1. What does this passage mainly discuss?
   A. The scarcity of manufactured goods.
   B. The value of scarce materials.
   C. The manufacturing of scarce goods.
   D. The cost of producing shoes.

2. According to the passage, what are the opportunity costs of an item?
   A. The amount of time and money spent in producing it.
   B. The opportunities a person has to buy it.
   C. The value of what could have been produced instead.
   D. The value of the resources used in its production.

3. According to the passage, what is the relationship between production and resources?
   A. Available resources stimulate production.
   B. Resources are totally independent of production.
   C. Production increases as resources increase.
   D. Production lessens the amount of available resources.

4. What determines the price of goods in a market economy?
   A. The cost of all elements in production.
   B. The cost of not making other goods.
   C. The efficiency of the manufacturing process.
   D. The quantity of materials supplied.

5. Which of the following examples BEST reflects a cost to society as defined in the passage?
   A. A family buying a dog.
   B. Eating in a restaurant instead of at home.
   C. Using land for a house instead of a park.
   D. Staying at home instead of going to school.

Words & Expressions

1. **supersonic** *adj*. 超音波的
   e. g. a supersonic plane 超音速飞机

2. **use up** 用完，耗尽
   e. g. He used up his last dollar to see the movies. 他把他最后的一块钱花在看电影上了。

3. **ultimately** *adv.* 最后,终于

   e. g. We hope ultimately to be able to buy a house of our own. 我们希望最终能够自己买一所房子。

4. **take into account** 重视,考虑

   e. g. We will certainly take your feelings into account. 我们当然会考虑到你的感情。

5. **mechanism** *n.* 机制,机构

   e. g. the mechanism of government 政府机构

6. **bid** *vt. & vi.* (在拍卖中)竞出高价,哄价,抬价;投标竞争

   e. g. bid money for sth. 为某物哄价

   Three firms bid for the contracts on the new buildings. 有 3 家公司投标竞争承包新楼工程。

7. **correspondingly** *adv.* 相对地;对照地

Notes

1. The true cost of, say, the construction of a supersonic jet is the value of the schools and refrigerators that will never be built as a result. 比方说,制造超音速喷气机的真正代价就是学校没有资金建设,冰箱缺乏资金生产。

2. In deciding how to use resources most effectively to satisfy the wants of the community, this opportunity cost must ultimately be taken into account. 在决定如何最有效地利用资源满足社会需求的时候,必须最终考虑到机会成本。

3. In a market economy the price of goods and the quantity supplied depend on the cost of making it, and that cost, ultimately, is the cost of not making other goods. 在市场经济中,商品的价格和供给数量决定于该商品的生产成本,而这一成本,最终是以不生产其他商品为代价的。

Key to the Exercises

1. B   2. C   3. D   4. B   5. C

Unit

7

Passage 1

Directions

There are 10 questions after the passage. Go over the passage quickly and answer the questions in the given time.

For questions 1 – 7, mark

Y (for YES)   if the statement agrees with the information given in the passage;

N (for NO)   if the statement contradicts the information given in the passage;

NG (for NOT GIVEN) if the information is not given in the passage.

For questions 8 – 10, complete the sentences with the information given in the passage.

How to Be a Leader

What motivates people to work and to achieve? What circumstances create an environment in which some people achieve and others do not? Does motivation come from within or does it come from others—from leaders or managers? Can you motivate the unmotivated? Does it have to involve money? Why is it that some work teams achieve and others do not? Is it that the better work unit has better people? If this is so, then does that mean that the better work unit would succeed whether they were led or not?

Exactly leadership.

Leadership is an essential organizational resource which should be systematically planned, specified, prepared and developed.

Leadership is a complex process by which a person influences others to accomplish a mission, task, or objective and directs the organization in a way that makes it more cohesive and coherent. Leadership makes people want to achieve high goals and objectives,

Being considered a leader in our society is the ultimate compliment. "Leadership has become the universal vitamin C pill," says psychologist David Campbell of the Center for Creative Leadership in Colorado Springs, Colo. "People seem to want megadoses (维生素等的大剂量)."

No wonder. Leadership bestows power, commands respect and, most importantly, fosters achievement. Unlike vitamins, though, leadership skills can't be easily gulped down. They must be carefully cultivated.

Contrary to popular belief, most good leaders are made, not born. They hone (用磨刀石磨) their skills in their everyday lives. If one has the desire and willpower, then they can become an effective leader. Good leaders develop through a never-ending process of self-study, education, training, and experience.

But which do they cultivate? How do they (and how can you) get others to follow?

Always give credit

Many leaders note that the most efficient way to get a good performance from others is to treat them like heroes. Giving public credit to someone who has earned it is the best leadership technique in the world. It is also an act of generosity that's never forgotten.

Giving credit is more effective than even the most constructive criticism, which often hurt rather than helps. Kenneth Blanchard, co-author of the One-minute Manager, agrees. "Catch people doing something right!" he says. Then tell everyone about it. The loyalty you will generate is arguably the most important currency a leader has.

Take informed risks

"The best leaders know that taking a risk is not a thoughtless exercise," says management consultant Marilyn Machlowitz. "Sky divers don't go up in an airplane without checking the parachutes beforehand."

Because the idea of risk also carries with it the possibility of failure, many of us tend to wait for others to take charge. But if you want to be a leader, you must learn to fail—and not die a thousand deaths. Pick yourself up and start all over again.

Show the way

In 1965, Lee Ducat was a Philadelphia homemaker with a child who had just been found to have diabetes (糖尿病). Ducat tried to reach out to other mothers of diabetic kids, but at first no one wanted to talk.

Finally Ducat managed to find three other mothers willing to share their experience, and from that beginning she went on to found and lead the Juvenile Diabetes foundation, which currently has 150 chapters worldwide. Ducat also formed the National Disease Research Interchange, which procures human tissues for vital research. Lee Ducat's secret? Being a role model.

"Have you ever noticed that if you smile at people, they smile back?" she asks. "Well, if you're giving, people want to give right back. If you're sure-footed, they want to follow in your footsteps. If you're confident about reaching a goal, others echo that confidence and try to achieve it for you."

"The best thing you can do is to get followers to mirror your actions by being what you wish them to be."

Keep the faith

Successful leaders often say that if you trust others to do well, they will. If, on the other hand, you believe your people will fail, they will probably meet your expectations as well. Business-man-philanthropist W. Clement Stone suggests that you express your faith in a letter. He says the executive who writes of faith in and commitment to his salespeople can motivate them to break records; the teacher who writes individual notes of encouragement to students can lead them to extraordinary heights. Having faith in someone gives him self-confidence and pleasure. It may sound corny(过时的), but the experts agree it works.

Get a compass

People don't follow leaders who lack direction. Estee Lauder, founder of the cosmetics company, has led thousands of employees to great success. She claims that every business leader she knows puts a clear picture of what he wants to achieve in his mind and stays focused on the picture. "People want to follow those who promise—and deliver—success," she says.

Act the part

Good leaders have learned to sound and look like winners. They may sometimes doubt themselves, but they don't show it, says management consultant Paula Bern. They act as if they know where they're going.

Leaders also know that appearance and manners count. They are usually pleasant to be with; their speech is polished, their demeanor unruffled and assured.

Be competent

Knowledge is power, the saying goes, and the best leaders know that their savvy and proficiency are part of their charisma(个人魅力). Competence galvanizes people, and will make them look to you for guidance and directions.

Foster enthusiasm

"When people understand the importance of work, they lend their mental strengths," says Lee Ducat. "But, oh, when they get excited about the work, all their energy gets poured into the job. That's a massive force! The best way to generate excitement? Be enthusiastic yourself and it's contagious. "

Delegate

Chris Alger, a young, divorced mother, was too busy getting her own life together to think about leading anyone anywhere. But one day she noticed how many people were going hungry in downtown Miami. She returned that evening with a friend and 20 bologna sandwiches. The next night, she brought more sandwiches. She began preparing soup and coffee, and soon it became apparent that she and her friend couldn't handle everything. "I'd never mobilized people before, but I had no choice," says Alger. "Others were depending on me to act. I picked up the phone. "

She became so visible that a local newspaper and television station did stories on her. The power of the press produced other volunteers, among them a philanthropist who donated money, contacts and organizational skills.

Now volunteers make and serve 500 sandwiches a day, as well as gallons of soup.

"It's not just me doing all this," Alger stresses. "So many have become involved. I couldn't do it alone. "

Exactly. Leadership.

> **Approximate Length: 1,127 words**
> **Suggested reading time: 8 minutes**
> **How fast do you read?** _____

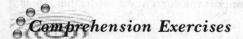

Comprehension Exercises

Complete the following exercises without referring back to the passage you have read.

1. This passage mainly discusses some qualities a leader should possess.
2. The psychologist David Campbell compared leadership to Vitamin C pills.
3. Most good leaders are not cultivated but born naturally.
4. The best leaders should always take informed risks.
5. Ducat is a case in point to show how to keep faith in others.
6. As a leader, it is your responsibility to put a clear picture of the future for the team.
7. Competence will make you go to your ultimate success.
8. The best way to generate enthusiasm is to _____.
9. Chris Alger is a divorced mother who is too busy _____.
10. The reason why so many people mentioned in the passage are successful is that they have some kind of ability called _____.

Words & Expressions

1. **compliment** *n.* 赞扬，敬意

   e. g. pay sb. a compliment；pay a compliment to sb.（on sth.）恭维某人

2. **bestow** *vt.* bestow on /upon（正式）给予，授予，赐予

   e. g. honors bestowed on him by the president 总统授予他的荣誉

3. **cultivate** *vt.* 耕种，培养

   e. g. cultivate the mind 修养心性

4. **currency** *n.* 货币；通用，流通

   e. g. give currency to 使流行；使传播

5. **parachute** *n.* 降落伞

6. **compass** *n.* 指南针；（喻）明确的目标

7. **proficiency** *n.* 熟练，精通

   e. g. proficiency in English 精通英语

Notes

1. Giving public credit to someone who has earned it is the best leadership technique in the world. It is also an act of generosity that's never forgotten. 当人们取得成就时，当众赞扬他们，这或许是世界上最佳的领导技巧，也是一种让人铭记于心的慷慨行为。

   give credit to sb. 称赞某人

2. The loyalty you will generate is arguably the most important currency a leader has. 由此激发的忠诚很可能成为一个领导者最重要的成功保证。

3. But if you want to be a leader, you must learn to fail—and not die a thousand deaths. Pick yourself up and start all over again. 如果你想成为一位领导者，你就必须学会面对失败——百折不挠，即使跌倒了也要再爬起来，一切从零开始。

4. The power of the press produced other volunteers, among them a philanthropist who donated money, contacts and organizational skills. 这种舆论的力量引来了其他志愿者，他们中有一个是慈善家，他捐赠了许多钱，还介绍了一些社会关系并传授了许多组织技巧。

Key to the Exercises

1. Y   2. Y   3. N   4. N   5. N   6. Y   7. NG   8. be enthusiastic yourself

9. getting her own life together to think about leading anyone anywhere   10. leadership

Passage 2

Directions

In this section, there is a passage with 10 blanks. You are required to select one word for each blank from a list of choices given in a word bank following the passage. Read the passage though carefully before making your choices. Each choice in the bank is identified by a letter. Please choose the corresponding letter for each item. You may not use any of the words in the bank more than once.

Reading Is Leaving Us Farther and Farther

If our society ever needed a reading renaissance (复兴), it's now. The National Endowment for the Arts released "Reading at Risk" last year, a study showing that adult reading __1__ have dropped 10 percentage points in the past decade, with the steepest drop among those 18 to 24. "Only one half of young people read a book of any kind in 2002. We set the bar almost on the ground. If you read one short story in a teenager magazine, that would have __2__ ," laments a director of research and analysis. He __3__ the loss of readers to the booming world of technology, which attracts would-be leisure readers to E-mail, IM chats, and video games and leaves them with no time to cope with a novel.

"These new forms of media undoubtedly have some benefits," says Steven Johnson, author of Everything Bad Is Good for You. Video games __4__ problem-solving skills; TV shows promote mental gymnastics by __5__ viewers to follow complex story lines. But books offer experience that can't be gained from these other sources, from __6__ vocabulary to stretching the imagination. "If they're not reading at all," says Johnson, "that's a huge problem."

In fact, fewer kids are reading for pleasure. According to data __7__ last week from the National Center for Educational Statistic's long-term trend assessment, the number of 17-year-olds who reported never or hardly ever reading for fun __8__ from 9 percent in 1984 to 19 percent in 2004. At the same time, the __9__ of 17-year-olds who read daily dropped from 31 to 22.

This slow but steady retreat from books has not yet taken a toll on reading ability. Scores for the nation's youth have __10__ constant over the past two decades (with an encouraging upswing among 9-year-olds). But given the strong apparent correlation between pleasure reading and reading skills, this means poorly for the future.

Approximate Length：312 words

A. percent	B. remained	C. rose
D. rates	E. percentage	F. counted
G. relieved	H. present	I. Believing
J. released	K. forcing	L. improve
M. Styles	N. building	O. attributes

1. _____ 2. _____ 3. _____ 4. _____ 5. _____
6. _____ 7. _____ 8. _____ 9. _____ 10. _____

Words & Expressions

1. **release** *vt.* 释放，此处意为出版，发表
   e. g. release sb. from the prison 从监狱释放出来
2. **steep** *adj.* 陡峭的，险峻的，此处意为下降幅度最大的
3. **boom** *n.* 景气，商业繁荣期
   e. g. baby boom 婴儿生育高峰期
4. **gymnastics** *n.* 体操

Notes

1. If you read one short story in a teenager magazine，that would have counted. 即使你只读了青少年杂志上的一篇小故事，那也被计算在内。
2. He attributes the loss of readers to the booming world of technology，which attracts would-be leisure readers to E-mail，IM chats，and video games and leaves them with no time to cope with a novel. 他把读书者数量的减少归因于科技的繁荣，一部分潜在的为消遣而读书的读者被电子邮件、网上聊天及电子游戏所吸引，而没有时间读小说。
   attribute...to... 把……归因于……
3. But books offer experience that can't be gained from these other sources，from building vocabulary to stretching the imagination. 但是书本能提供从其他资源所无法获得的东西：扩大词汇量及提高想象力。
4. This slow but steady retreat from books has not yet taken a toll on reading ability. 读书人数缓慢而稳定的下降还没有引起人们对于阅读能力的关注。
   take a toll on ... 对……敲响警钟
5. But given the strong apparent correlation between pleasure reading and reading skills，this means poorly for the future. 但考虑到消遣阅读和阅读能力之间的紧密关系，这（指读书人数的减

少）对未来很不利。

　　given 考虑到,鉴于

Key to the Exercises

1. D　　2. F　　3. O　　4. L　　5. K　　6. N　　7. J　　8. C　　9. E　　10. B

Passage 3

Directions

The passage is followed by some questions or unfinished statements. For each of them there are four choices marked A, B, C and D. You should decide on the best choice after reading.

The Importance of C. V. in Job Application

There is a new type of small advertisement becoming increasingly common in newspaper classified columns. It is sometimes placed among "situations vacant", although it does not offer anyone a job, and sometimes it appears among "situations wanted", although it is not placed by someone looking for a job, either. What it does is to offer help in applying for a job.

"Contact us before writing your application", or "Make use of our long experience in preparing your curriculum vitae or job history" is how it is usually expressed. The growth and apparent success of such a specialized service is, of course, a reflection on the current high levels of unemployment. It is also an indication of the growing importance of the curriculum vitae (or job history), with the suggestion that it may now qualify as an art form in its own right.

There was a time when job seekers simply wrote letters of application. "Just put down your name, address, age and whether you have passed any exams" was about the average level of advice offered to young people applying for their first jobs when I left school. The letter was really just for openers, it was explained, everything else could and should be saved for the interview. And in those days of full employment the technique worked. The letter proved that you could write and were available for work. Your eager face and intelligent replies did the rest.

Later, as you moved up the ladder, something slightly more sophisticated was called for. The advice then was to put something in the letter which would distinguish you from the rest. It might be the aggressive approach. "Your search is over. I am the person you are looking for", was a widely used trick that occasionally succeeded. Or it might be some special feature specially designed for the job interview.

There is no doubt, however, that it is increasing number of applicants with university education at all points in the process of engaging staff that has led to the greater importance of the curriculum vitae.

Approximate Length: 344 words

1. The new type of advertisement which is appearing in newspaper columns _____.
   A. informs job hunters of the opportunities available
   B. promises to offer useful advice to those looking for employment
   C. divides available jobs into various types
   D. informs employers of the people available for work

2. Nowadays a demand for this specialized type of service has been created because _____.
   A. there is a lack of jobs available for artistic people
   B. there are so many top-level jobs available
   C. there are so many people out of work
   D. the job history is considered to be a work of art

3. In the past it was expected that first job hunters would _____.
   A. write an initial letter giving their life history
   B. pass some exams before applying for a job
   C. have no qualifications other than being able to read and write
   D. keep any detailed information until they obtained an interview

4. Later, as one went on to apply for more important jobs, one was advised to include in the letter _____.
   A. something that would distinguish one from other applicants
   B. hinted information about the personality of the applicant
   C. one's advantages over others in applying for the job
   D. an occasional trick with the aggressive approach

5. The curriculum vitae has become such an important document because _____.
   A. there has been an increase in the number of jobs advertised
   B. there has been an increase in the number of applicants with degrees
   C. jobs are becoming much more complicated nowadays
   D. the other processes of applying for jobs are more complicated

Words & Expressions

1. **vita** *n.* 个人简历,生活,生命,传记,自传 *pl.* vitae

   e. g. curriculum vitae 履历书

2. **apply** *vt.* 申请,应用;*vi.* 申请,适用;专心,努力

   e. g. apply a theory to practice 把理论应用于实践

   apply for 申请;请求

   apply oneself to 致力于,集中精力做某事

3. **sophisticated** *adj.* 老练的,老于世故的;精密的,复杂的

4. **aggressive** *adj.* 好斗的,敢作敢为的,有闯劲的,侵略性的

   e. g. an aggressive foreign policy 侵略性的外交政策

   Martin is too aggressive. 马丁太盛气凌人了。

Notes

1. situations vacant 招聘栏目; situations wanted 求职栏目

2. The growth and apparent success of such a specialized service is, of course, a reflection on the current high levels of unemployment. 这种专业服务的出现和发展反映了当今的高失业率。

3. The letter was really just for openers, it was explained, everything else could and should be saved for the interview. 求职信不必写得太详细,应该在得到面试机会时再表述更多细节。

4. ... it is increasing number of applicants with university education at all points in the process of engaging staff that has led to the greater importance of the curriculum vitae. 越来越多具有大学教育背景的求职者的加入,使得写好个人履历显得尤为重要。

Key to the Exercises

1. B   2. C   3. D   4. A   5. B

Passage 4

Directions

The passage is followed by some questions or unfinished statements. For each of them there are four choices marked A, B, C and D. You should decide on the best choice after reading.

Women and Fashion

If women are mercilessly exploited（剥削）year after year，they have only themselves to blame．Because they tremble at the thought of being seen in public in clothes that are out of fashion，and they are always taken advantage of by the designers and the big stores．Clothes which have been worn only a few times have to be put aside because of the change of fashion．When you come to think of it，only a woman is capable of standing in front of a wardrobe packed full of clothes and announcing sadly that she has nothing to wear．

Changing fashions are nothing more than the intentional creation of waste．Many women spend vast sums of money each year to replace clothes that have hardly been worn．Women who cannot afford to throw away clothing in this way，waste hours of their time altering the dresses they have．Skirts are lengthened or shortened；neck-lines are lowered or raised，and so on．

No one can claim that the fashion industry contributes anything really important to society．Fashion designers are rarely concerned with vital things like warmth，comfort and durability（耐用）．They are only interested in outward appearance and they take advantage of the fact that women will put up with any amount of discomfort，as long as they look right．There can hardly be a man who hasn't at some time in his life smiled at the sight of a woman shaking in a thin dress on a winter day，or delicately picking her way through deep snow in high-heeled shoes．

When comparing men and women in the matter of fashion，the conclusions to be drawn are obvious．Do the constantly changing fashions of women's clothes，one wonders，reflect basic qualities of inconstancy and instability? Men are too clever to let themselves be cheated by fashion designers．Do their unchanging styles of dress reflect basic qualities of stability and reliability? That is for you to decide．

Approximate Length：330 words

1. Designers and big stores always make money _____．
   A. by mercilessly exploiting women workers in the clothing industry
   B. because they are capable of predicting new fashions
   C. by constantly changing the fashions in women's clothing
   D. because they attach great importance to quality in women's clothing
2. To the writer, the fact that women alter their old-fashioned dresses is seen as _____．
   A. a waste of money
   B. a waste of time

C. an expression of taste   D. an expression of creativity

3. The writer would be less critical if fashion designers placed more stress on the _____ of clothing.

   A. cost   B. appearance   C. comfort   D. suitability

4. According to the passage, which of the following statements is TRUE?

   A. New fashions in clothing are created for the commercial exploitation of women.

   B. The constant changes in women's clothing reflect their strength of character.

   C. The fashion industry makes an important contribution to society.

   D. Fashion designs should not be encouraged since they are only welcomed by women.

5. By saying "the conclusions to be drawn are obvious" (Para. 4), the writer means that _____.

   A. women's inconstancy in their choice of clothing is often laughed at

   B. women are better able to put up with discomfort

   C. men are also exploited greatly by fashion designers

   D. men are more reasonable in the matter of fashion

Words & Expressions

1. **mercilessly** *adv.* 残酷无情地

   mercifully *adv.* 幸运地

2. **contribute** *vt.* 捐助，捐献，贡献；投稿

   e. g. contribute food and clothing for the refugees 向难民捐赠食品和衣物

   Drink contributed to his ruin. 酗酒促使他毁灭。

3. **delicately** *adv.* 优美地，微妙地

   delicate *adj.* 优美的

   e. g. The international situation is very delicate at present. 当前的国际形势十分微妙。

4. **reflect** *vt.* 反射；反映；反省，细想

   e. g. Many newspapers reflect the opinions of the children. 许多报纸都反映了儿童们的看法。

5. **inconstancy** *n.* 反复无常，出尔反尔

Notes

1. Because they tremble at the thought of being seen in public in clothes that are out of fashion, they are always taken advantage of by the designers and the big stores. 因为妇女们害怕被看见在公共场合穿过时的服装，她们频频利用服装设计师和大商场。

2. ...only a woman is capable of standing in front of a wardrobe packed full of clothes and announcing sadly that she has nothing to wear. 只有女人能站在装满衣服的衣柜前悲哀地说没有衣服穿。

3. Changing fashions are nothing more than the intentional creation of waste. 改变服装的式样

不过是有意地制造浪费。

4. Fashion designers are rarely concerned with vital things like warmth, comfort and durability. 服装设计师对衣服的关键因素如是否保暖、舒适、耐穿等很少考虑。

Key to the Exercises

1. C   2. B   3. C   4. A   5. D

Passage 1

Trust Me, I Am a Robot

Robot safety: as robots move into homes and offices, ensuring that they do not injure people will be vital. But how?

The incident

In 1981 Kenji Urada, a 37-year-old Japanese factory worker, climbed over a safety fence at a Kawasaki plant to carry out some maintenance work on a robot. In his haste, he failed to switch the robot off properly. Unable to sense him, the robot's powerful hydraulic arm kept on working and accidentally pushed the engineer into a grinding machine. His death made Urada the first recorded victim to die at the hands of a robot.

This gruesome industrial accident would not have happened in a world in which robot behavior was governed by the Three Laws of Robotics drawn up by Isaac Asimov, a science-fiction writer. The laws appeared in *I Am a Robot*, a book of short stories published in 1950 that inspired a recent Hollywood film. But decades later the laws, designed to prevent robots from harming people either through action or inaction, remain in the realm of fiction.

Indeed, despite the introduction of improved safety mechanisms, robots have claimed many more victims since 1981. Over the years people have been crushed, hit on the head, welded and even had molten aluminum poured over them by robots. Last year there were 77 robot-related accidents in Britain alone, according to the Health and Safety Executive.

More related issues

With robots now poised to emerge from their industrial cages and to move into homes and workplaces, roboticists are concerned about the safety implications beyond the factory floor. To address these concerns, leading robot experts have come together to try to find ways to prevent robots from harming people. Inspired by the Pugwash Conferences—an international group of scientists, academics and activists founded in 1957 to campaign for the non-proliferation of nuclear weapons—the new group of robo-ethicists met earlier this year in Genoa, Italy, and announced their initial findings in March at the European Robotics Symposium in Palermo, Sicily.

"Security, safety and sex are the big concerns," says Henrik Christensen, chairman of the European Robotics Network at the Swedish Royal Institute of Technology in Stockholm, and one of the organizers of the new robo-ethics group. Should robots that are strong enough or heavy enough to crush people be allowed into homes? Is "system malfunction" a justifiable defiance for a robotic fighter plane that contravenes the Geneva Convention and mistakenly fires on innocent villains? And should robotic sex dolls resembling children be legally allowed?

"These questions may seem esoteric but in the next few years they will become increasingly relevant," says Dr. Christensen. According to the United Nations Economic Commission for Europe's World Robotics Survey, in 2002 the number of domestic and service robots more than tripled, nearly surpassing their industrial counterparts. By the end of 2003 there were more than 600,000 robot vacuum cleaners and lawn mowers—a figure predicted to rise to more than 4 times by the end of the next year. Japanese industrial firms are racing to build humanoid robots to act as domestic helpers for the elderly, and South Korea has set a goal that 100% of households should have domestic robots by 2020. "In light of all this, it is crucial that we start to think about safety and ethical guidelines now," says Dr. Christensen.

Difficulties

So what exactly is being done to protect us from these mechanical menaces? "Not enough," says Blay Whiteby, an artificial intelligence expert at the University of Sussex in England. "This is hardly surprising given that the field of 'safety-critical computing' is barely a decade old," he says. But things are changing, and researchers are increasingly taking an interest in trying to make robots safer.

"Regulating the behavior of robots is going to become more difficult in the future, since they will increasingly have self-learning mechanisms built into them," says Gianmarco Veruggio, a roboticist in Italy. "As a result, their behavior will become impossible to predict fully," he says, "since they will not be behaving in predefined ways but will learn new behavior as they go."

Then there is the question of unpredictable failures. What happens if a robot's motors stop working, or it suffers a system failure just as it is performing heart surgery or handing you a cup of hot coffee? "You can, of course, build in redundancy by adding backup systems," says Hirochika Inoue, a veteran roboticist at the University of Tokyo who is now an adviser to Japan Society for the Promotion of Science. "But this guarantees nothing," he says, "One hundred percent safety is impossible through technology," says Dr. Inoue. "This is because ultimately no matter how thorough you are, you cannot anticipate the unpredictable nature of human behavior," he says.

Legal problems

So where does this leave Asimov's Three Laws of Robotics? "They were a narrative device, and were never actually meant to work in the real world," says Dr. Whitby. Let alone the fact that the laws require the robot to have some form of human-like intelligence, which robots still lack, the laws themselves don't actually work very well. Indeed, Asimov repeatedly knocked them down in his robot stores, showing time and again how these seemingly watertight rules could produce unintended consequences.

"In any case," says Dr. Inoue, "the laws really just encapsulate commonsense principles that are already applied to the design of most modern appliances, both domestic and industrial." Every toaster, lawn mower and mobile phone is designed to minimize the risk of causing injury, yet people still manage to electrocute themselves, lose fingers or fall out of windows in an effort to get a better signal. At the very least, robots must meet the rigorous safety standards that cover existing products. The question is whether new, robot-specific rules are needed, and, if so, what they should say.

"Making sure robots are safe will be critical," says Colin Angle of Robot, which has sold over 2m "Roomba" household-vacuuming robots. But he argues that his firm's robots are, in fact, much safer than some popular toys. But what he believes is that robot is just like other home appliances that deserves no special treatment.

Robot safety is likely to appear in the civil courts as a matter of product liability. "When the first robot carpet-sweeper sucks up a boy, who will be to blame?" asks John Hallam, a professor at the University of Southern Denmark in Odense. If a robot is autonomous and capable of learning, can its designer be held responsible for all its actions? Today the answer to these questions is generally "yes". But as robots grow in complexity it will become a lot less clear cut, he says.

However, the idea that general-purpose robots, capable of learning, will become widespread is wrong, suggests Mr. Angle. It is more likely, he believes, that robots will be relatively dumb machines designed for particular tasks. Rather than a humanoid robot maid, "it's going to be a heterogeneous swarm of robots that will take care of the house," he says.

> **Approximate Length: 1,172 words**
> **Suggested reading time: 8 minutes**
> **How fast do you read?** _____

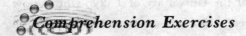

Comprehension Exercises

Complete the following exercises without referring back to the passage you have read.

1. This passage is mainly about the benefits of developing robots and how people are going to get used to living with robots in their office and home.

2. The Three Laws of Robotics mentioned in this passage only existed in a book of short stories.

3. Although people have realized the danger of robots and begun to introduce and improve the safety mechanisms, there is still increasing number of people dying at the hands of robots since 1981.

4. It can be inferred from this passage that the Pugwash Conference and the meeting in Genoa, Italy had come up with similar measures against potential dangers.

5. As Henrick Christensen pointed out, three big concerns related to robots were security, safety and sex.

6. According to the passage, East Asia is more likely to have more problems related to robot than western countries because they have a more ambitious plan for robot development.

7. With advancement in the field of artificial intelligence, it will be easier to regulate the behavior of robots in the future.

8. To avoid unpredictable failures, Hirochika Inoue suggests building in _____ by adding backup systems, but he also points out it might not guarantee everything.

9. There will be indeed unpredictable events; however, people believe that at least, robots must meet the rigorous safety standards that cover _____.

10. People believe that though it is possible that there will be more robots handling particular tasks, the general-purpose robots which are _____ will not be possible.

Words & Expressions

1. **maintenance** *n.* 维持或被维持，保养

   e.g. carry out some maintenance work on a robot 对机器人进行保养维修

2. **victim** *n.* 牺牲者，受害或遇难的人，动物等

3. **malfunction** *n.* 发生故障；*vi.* 发生故障，未起作用

4. **appliance** *n.* 工具，器具，用具

   e.g. household appliances 家用器具

5. **contravene** *vt.* （正式）违反（法律、法规）；与……冲突

   e.g. Milk from an unhealthy cow may contravene public health regulations. 不健康奶牛产的奶会违反公共卫生规定。

6. **triple** *vt.* & *vi.* 使成为三倍

7. **surpass** *vt.* 超越，凌驾，胜过

   e.g. surpass the expectations 比期望的更好

8. **in (the) light of ...** 借助，按照，根据

   e.g. In the light of the new evidence, it was decided to take the manufacturers to court. 根据新的证据，决定向法院控告那些制造商。

9. **ethical** *adj.* 道德的，伦理的，道德问题的

   e.g. ethical questions 道德问题

10. **menace** *n.* 危险，威胁 *vt.* 威胁，恐吓

    e.g. a menace to public safety 危害公共安全

11. **autonomous** *adj.* （指州或邦等）自治的，自主的，自由的

Notes

1. To address these concerns, leading robot experts have come together to try to find ways to prevent robots from harming people. 为了解决这些人们关注的问题，机器人领域的首席专家们聚集在一起来研究避免机器人伤人的方案。

2. "This is because ultimately no matter how thorough you are, you cannot anticipate the unpredictable nature of human behavior." he says. 他说："这是因为不管你多仔细，你总不能完全估计到各种不可预料的人类行为。"

3. ... showing time and again how these seemingly watertight rules could produce unintended consequences. ……（这样做）是为了反复证明这些表面上无漏洞的规则可能会造成意想不到的后果。

4. "In any case," says Dr. Inoue, "the laws really just encapsulate commonsense principles that are already applied to the design of most modern appliances, both domestic and industrial." Inoue 博士说："在任何情况下，法律只是规定一些常识性的规则，这些规则适用于大部分的现代器具，包括家用的和工业上使用的器具。"

5. At the very least, robots must meet the rigorous safety standards that cover existing products. 至少，机器人必须达到现存产品中所规定的严格的安全标准。

Key to the Exercises

1. N   2. Y   3. Y   4. NG   5. Y   6. NG   7. N
8. redundancy   9. existing products   10. capable of learning

Passage 2

> **Directions**
>
> In this section, there is a passage with 10 blanks. You are required to select one word for each blank from a list of choices given in a word bank following the passage. Read the passage though carefully before making your choices. Each choice in the bank is identified by a letter. Please choose the corresponding letter for each item. You may not use any of the words in the bank more than once.

The Automobile Has Changed Our Life Style

The automobile has probably changed people's way of life more than any other invention of the last century. More than ___1___ lights, television, air travel, or even ___2___, automobiles have changed where people live and work, how they make a living, and even how they find a mate.

Before there were cars, people ___3___ traveled on foot or by horse and buggy (轻便马车) over unpaved roads. Whether they lived in the city or the ___4___, they rarely went farther than a few miles from home, they saw the same people and places year after year.

The car opened up whole new worlds. Roads were paved, and ___5___ went to see different parts of the country. Some decided to stay. People with cars could live farther from their jobs and so the age of commuting (乘班车上下班) began. New suburbs ___6___ up around the cities. And millions of Americans made a living by manufacturing, selling, or ___7___ cars.

As more people got cars, young people began driving them. No longer was courtship confined to the girl's front porch, under the ___8___ eyes of her parents. The automobiles began to sexual ___9___.

Some people believe that commuting, ___10___ life, and courting in cars are mixed blessings. Whether the changes are good or bad, they seem to be here to say.

Approximate Length: 239 words

A. computers   B. generally   C. electric
D. country   E. motorists   F. repairing
G. revolution   H. watchful   I. operator
J. particularly   K. electronic   L. sprang
M. bring   N. suburban   O. solution

1. _____   2. _____   3. _____   4. _____   5. _____
6. _____   7. _____   8. _____   9. _____   10. _____

Words & Expressions

1. **spring** (**sprang**, **sprung**) *vi.* 跃出,突然活动
   spring up 出现,迅速长出
   e.g. New buildings sprang up everywhere in this small town. 这座小城镇处处盖起了新的大楼。
2. **courtship** *n.* 恋爱期
3. **porch** *n.* 门厅,门道
4. **confine** *vt.* 限制
   be confined to 把……限制于
   e.g. He is only confined to talking about his job, not his personal affairs. 只允许他谈他的工作,而非他的私事。
5. **blessing** *n.* 幸运,福气
   e.g. a mixed blessing 有利亦有弊的事情

Notes

No longer was courtship confined to the girl's front porch, under the ... eyes of her parents. (由于汽车的发明)恋爱期间的约会不再局限于女孩家的前门廊了,而且也不再在父母的监视下进行了。
本句是一个由 no longer 位于句首而引导的倒装句。

Key to the Exercises

1. C   2. A   3. B   4. D   5. E   6. L   7. F   8. H   9. G   10. N

Passage 3

Directions

The passage is followed by some questions or unfinished statements. For each of them there are four choices marked A, B, C and D. You should decide on the best choice after reading.

Lincoln, an Unforgettable President

Lincoln was a strong executive who saved the government, saved the United States. He was a president who understood people, and, when time came to make decisions, he was willing to take the responsibility and make those decisions, no matter how difficult they were. He knew how to treat people and how to make a decision stick, and that's why he is regarded as such a great administrator.

Carl Sandburg and a lot of others have tried to make something out of Lincoln that he wasn't. He was a decent man, a good politician, and a great president, and they've tried to build up things that he never even thought about. I'll bet a dollar and a half that if you read Sandburg's biography of Lincoln, you'll find things put into Lincoln's mouth and mind that never even occurred to him. He was a good man who was in the place where he ought to have been at the time important events were taking place, but when they write about him as though he belongs in the pantheon(众神庙)of the gods, that's not the man he really was. He was the best kind of ordinary man, and when I say that he was an ordinary man, I mean that as high praise, not deprecation(强烈不赞成，反对). That's the highest praise you can give a man. He's one of the people and becomes distinguished in the service that he gives other people. He was one of the people, and he wanted to stay that way. And he was that way until the day he died. One of the reasons he was assassinated was because he didn't feel important enough to have the proper guards around him at Ford's Theatre.

Approximate Length: 300 words

1. According to the passage, Lincoln was _____.
   A. a man belonging in the pantheon of the gods

B. defied(藐视)by all the people

C. as ordinary as all the other people

D. a responsible person

2. What's the author's comment on Carl Sandburg's biography of Lincoln?

A. It's objective.   B. It's unfair to Lincoln.

C. It sang high praise of Lincoln.   D. It's widely read.

3. What's the author's attitude toward Lincoln?

A. admiring.   B. indifferent.   C. critical.   D. affectionate.

4. Which of the following titles suits the passage best?

A. Lincoln—an Ordinary Man.   B. Lincoln—a Great Politician.

C. Lincoln's Biography by Carl Sandburg.   D. How was Lincoln Assassinated?

5. In the author's opinion, an ordinary man _____.

A. is a mediocre(平庸的)person   B. can never become distinguished

C. indicates deprecation   D. can be used to praise a person

Words & Expressions

1. **executive** *n.* 执行者；行政长官；[美]最高行政官(指州长或总统)

      adj. 实行的，执行的，行政的

  e. g. The president of a company is an executive. 公司的经理是公司的管理者。

    an executive committee 执行委员会

2. **administration** *n.* 管理，经营；行政部门

  e. g. academic administration (高等学校)教务处；学术行政

3. **decent** *adj.* 正派的，端庄的；有分寸的；(服装)得体的

  e. g. decent language and decent behavior 高雅的谈吐和行为

4. **occur** *vi.* 发生，出现

  e. g. it occurs to sb. 浮现在某人的脑海中；被某人想到

5. **assassinate** *vt.* 暗杀，行刺；中伤，破坏(名誉等)

  e. g. assassinate a person's character 破坏一个人的名誉

Notes

1. He was a president who understood people, and, when time came to make decisions, he was willing to take the responsibility and make those decisions, no matter how difficult they were. 林肯是一个理解人民的总统，无论有多困难，当需要做出决定的时候他总是乐于承担责任。

2. He was a good man who was in the place where he ought to have been at the time important events were taking place, but when they write about him as though he belongs in the pantheon(众神庙)of the gods, that's not the man he really was. 林肯是一个好人，当有重大事件发生的时候他总在他应该在的位置，但是人们给他写传记的时候就好像他是位于众神之列而不

是一个真实的人。

3. One of the reasons he was assassinated was because he didn't feel important enough to have the proper guards around him at Ford's Theatre. 他被暗杀的原因之一就是他认为在福特剧院没必要在他周围配备适当的警力。

Key to the Exercises

1. D　　　2. C　　　3. A　　　4. A　　　5. D

Passage 4

Directions

The passage is followed by some questions or unfinished statements. For each of them there are four choices marked A, B, C and D. You should decide on the best choice after reading.

Make a Timely and Heartfelt Apology

It's never easy to admit you are in the wrong. Being human, we all need to know the art of apologizing. Look back with honesty and think how often you've judged roughly, said unkind things, pushed yourself ahead at the expense of a friend. Then count the occasions when you indicated clearly and truly that you were sorry. A bit frightening, isn't it? Frightening because some deep wisdom in us knows that when even a small wrong has been committed, some mysterious moral feeling is disturbed; and it stays out of balance until fault is acknowledged and regret expressed.

I remember a doctor friend, the late Clarence Lieb, telling me about a man who came to him with a variety of signs: headaches, insomnia（失眠）and stomach trouble. No physical cause could be found. Finally Dr. Lieb said to the man, "Unless you tell me what's worrying you, I can't help you." After some hesitation, the man confessed that, as executor of his father's will, he had been cheating his brother, who lived abroad of his inheritance. Then and there the wise old doctor made the man write to his brother asking forgiveness and enclosing a cheque as the first step in restoring their good relation. He then went with him to the mailbox in the corridor. As the letter disappeared, the man burst into tears. "Thank you," he said, "I think I'm cured. " And he was.

A heartfelt apology can not only heal a damaged relationship but also make it stronger. If you can think of someone who deserves an apology from you, someone you have wronged, or judged too roughly, or just neglected, do something about it right now.

Approximate Length: 274 words

1. When we have done something wrong, we should _____.
   A. look honest and think over the fault carefully
   B. escape from being disturbed
   C. admit the fault and express the regret
   D. forgive ourselves
2. What will happen if we have done something wrong?
   A. Our logic of thinking will be disturbed.   B. We shall be sad.
   C. We shall apologize at once.   D. Our moral balance will be disturbed.
3. What exactly was the patient's trouble?
   A. The losing of a friend.   B. Headaches, insomnia, and stomachs.
   C. Something wrong with his conscience.   D. Some unknown physical weakness.
4. What had the patient done to his brother?
   A. He had sent his brother abroad.
   B. He had been dishonest to his brother.
   C. He had given just a little share of the inheritance to his brother.
   D. He had been too busy to write to his brother.
5. The patient was cured by _____.
   A. writing a letter   B. crossing a cheque
   C. asking his brother to forgive him   D. mailing a letter

Words & Expressions

1. **at the expense of** 以……为代价,牺牲
   e. g. He became a brilliant scholar, but only at the expense of his health. 他成了一个卓越的学者,但却牺牲了健康。
2. **late** *adj.* 已故的
   e. g. the late president 已故的总统
3. **confess** *vt.* 认错,招供,承认
   e. g. He confessed that he had stolen the money. 他承认他偷了那笔钱。
4. **executor** *n.* (立遗嘱者所委托之)遗嘱执行人
5. **inheritance** *n.* 继承,遗传
6. **heal** *vt.* 治愈,痊愈

e. g. heal sb. of a disease 医治某人的病

Notes

1. Frightening because some deep wisdom in us knows that when even a small wrong has been committed, some mysterious moral feeling is disturbed; and it stays out of balance until fault is acknowledged and regret expressed. 我们之所以害怕是因为内心深处的理智告知我们，即使我们犯的错误很小，但道德良知却让我们感到不安，直到向对方承认了错误，表达了歉意，我们的心里才会平静。

2. Then and there the wise old doctor made the man write to his brother asking forgiveness and enclosing a cheque as the first step in restoring their good relation. 当时，这位聪明的老医生就让这个人给弟弟写了封信，请求原谅，并随信附上一张支票，以此作为恢复两人关系的第一步。

3. If you can think of someone who deserves an apology from you, someone you have wronged, or judged too roughly, or just neglected, do something about it right now. 如果你能记起你应该向某人道歉，你曾经冤枉了他，对他做出过草率的判断，或忽视了他，那么现在就采取行动吧（向他道歉吧）。

Key to the Exercises

1. C   2. D   3. C   4. B   5. C

Unit

9

Passage 1

Directions

There are 10 questions after the passage. Go over the passage quickly and answer
the questions in the given time.

For questions 1 – 7, mark

Y (for YES)   if the statement agrees with the information given in the passage;

N (for NO)   if the statement contradicts the information given in the passage;

NG (for NOT GIVEN) if the information is not given in the passage.

For questions 8 – 10, complete the sentences with the information given in the
passage.

The Greenhouse Effect

Earth's climate has been changing constantly over its 5-billion-year history.

Sometimes, the climate has warmed so that the oceans have risen and covered much of
the Earth. Each of the changes may seem extreme, but they usually occurred slowly over
many thousands of years.

Ancient climate history

The first people arrived in America between 15,000 and 30,000 years ago. During that
time, much of North America was covered by great ice sheets. Some 14,000 years ago, the
last ice sheet began to melt very quickly. By 7,000 years ago, the ice was gone.

This end to the ice ages caused big changes on the Earth. The changes caused many
kinds of plants and animals to die. For example, mastodons-elephant-like animals, and other
large mammals that preferred cold climates may not have been able to live in the warmer,

drier conditions.

The little ice age

Starting in the 14th century, Europeans lived through what is known as the "Little Ice Age." The Little Ice Age lasted for several hundred years. During the Little Ice Age, the advance of glaciers along with hard winters and famines caused some people to starve and others to leave their homes.

Recent climate history

The Earth has warmed about 1℉ in the last 100 years. And the four warmest years of the 20th century all happened in the 1990s. Periods of increased heat from the sun may have helped make the Earth warmer. But many of the world's leading climatologists (气候学家) think that the greenhouse gases people produce are making the Earth warmer, too.

Scientists think the sea has risen partly because of inching glaciers and sea ice. When some glaciers melt, they release water into the sea and make it higher than it was before. Scientists also think that warmer temperatures in the sea make it rise even more. Heat makes water expand. When the ocean expands, it takes up more space.

What might happen?

Scientists are not fortune-tellers. They don't know exactly what will happen in the future. But they can use special computer programs to find out how the climate may change in the years ahead. And the computer programs tell us that the Earth may continue to get warmer.

Together, the melting glaciers, rising seas, and computer models provide some good clues. They tell us that the Earth's temperature will probably continue to rise as long as we continue increasing the amount of greenhouse gases in the atmosphere.

Scientists have to think like detectives. They look for clues to help them understand how the world works. Then they investigate the clues to find evidence real—facts that can give them a better idea of what is going on. Here are some of the ways that scientists gather evidence about climate, both past and present.

Weather stations

Weather stations help us find out the temperature on the surface of the Earth. Weather stations use special thermometers that tell us the temperature. They can be set up almost anywhere on land. Weather stations also can tell us how fast the wind is moving and how much rain falls on the ground during a storm.

Weather balloons

Almost everyone likes balloons, including scientists! Weather balloons are released to float high up into the atmosphere. They carry special instruments that send all kinds of information about the weather back to people on the ground.

Ocean buoys

A buoy is an object that floats on water, and is often used to warn boats away from dangerous places in the ocean or on a river. But some buoys have special instruments on them. These buoys can tell us the temperature and other things about the conditions of the atmosphere.

Weather satellites

Humans send satellites into space to travel around the Earth. The satellites send back information to scientists on the ground. Some of the information they give us is about the weather and the Earth's temperature.

Ice cores

Some scientists who want to find out more about climate study ice for clues. Not just any ice—they are studying the ice from glaciers that have been around for a very long time. They cut pieces of ice and look for air bubbles that were trapped in the ice hundreds or even thousands of years ago. The air bubbles help them discover what the climate used to be like on Earth. The evidence they uncover is creating a historical record of regional temperatures and greenhouse gas concentrations dating back 160,000 years.

Sediment analyses

Sediment is the earth and rock that has built up in layers over time. Scientists are learning a great deal about past climate from studying these layers. Sediment layering provides information about where glaciers have been in the past. Ocean sediments provide a map of how ocean currents have flowed in the past. And fossilized pollen （粉末） found in sediment layers tells us about where different plants have grown in the past.

Tree rings

You can tell how old a tree is by counting its rings because it grows a new ring every year. Tree rings also can tell us how much precipitation （陡然下坠；猛冲） fell each year in the place where the tree lives.

What does all of this mean?

Weather stations, balloons, ocean buoys, and satellites tell us the Earth's temperature today. Ice cores, sediment layers, and tree rings tell us about what the Earth's climate has been like in the past. With this evidence, scientists are learning from how climate changes over time.

What are scientists still unsure about?

How do clouds respond to changes in temperature and precipitation? How do oceans transport heat? How do climate and intense weather events like hurricanes affect each other? As scientists try to answer these and other questions, they will discover many more clues about how the Earth's climate system works.

It may seem hard to believe that people can actually change the Earth's climate. But scientists think that the things people do that send greenhouse gases into the air are making our planet warmer.

Once, all climate changes occurred naturally. However, during the Industrial Revolution, we began altering our climate and environment through agricultural and industrial practices. The Industrial Revolution was a time when people began using machines to make life easier. It started more than 200 years ago and changed the way humans live. Before the Industrial Revolution, human activity released very few gases into the atmosphere, but now through population growth, fossil fuel burning, and deforestation, we are affecting the mixture of gases in the atmosphere.

Since the Industrial Revolution, the need for energy to run machines has steadily increased. Some energy, like the energy you need to do your homework, comes from the food you eat. But other energy, like the energy that makes cars run and much of the energy used to light and heat our homes, comes from fuels like coal and oil-fossil fuels. Burning these fuels releases greenhouse gases.

> Approximate Length: 1,146 words
> Suggested reading time: 8 minutes
> How fast do you read? _____

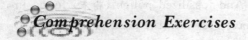

Comprehension Exercises

Complete the following exercises without referring back to the passage you have read.

1. The passage gives a general description of ancient climate history.
2. The Little Ice Age lasted for several years.
3. The Earth's temperature usually rises half a degree every century.
4. With the help of computer programs, scientists have predicted that the earth will continue to get warmer in the future.
5. Weather stations can not only tell us about wind speed, but also about rainfall.
6. Both weather balloons and ocean buoys can collect information about the temperature.
7. Ice Cores are only useful for giving us information about the current weather conditions.

8. Scientists can figure out where glaciers have been in the past through _____

_____.

9. Scientists believe that the things people do that send _____ gases into the air are making our planet warmer.

10. The need for energy to run machines has steadily increased since the _____.

Words & Expressions

1. **famine** *n.* 饥荒
2. **fortune-teller** *n.* 给人算命的人
3. **bubble** *n.* 气泡,泡沫
   e. g. blow bubbles 吹泡泡
4. **uncover** *vt.* 发现,破获,揭露;揭开……的盖子
   e. g. uncover the plot 揭露阴谋
5. **intense** *adj.* 强烈的;激烈的
   e. g. intense affection 热烈的感情;intense competition 激烈的竞争
6. **hurricane** *n.* 飓风;风暴
7. **deforestation** *n.* 森林的砍伐殆尽

Notes

1. During the Little Ice Age, the advance of glaciers along with hard winters and famines caused some people to starve and others to leave their homes. 在冰川期,伴随着严冬而来的冰川移动及饥荒使一些人饿死,还有些人被迫离开家乡。

2. When some glaciers melt, they release water into the sea and make it higher than it was before. 当冰川融化时,融化的水流入大海使海面比以前上升。

3. They carry special instruments that send all kinds of information about the weather back to people on the ground. 他们配备特殊的仪器,这种仪器可以将有关天气的信息发送给地面上的人。

4. Before the Industrial Revolution, human activity released very few gases into the atmosphere, but now through population growth, fossil fuel burning, and deforestation, we are affecting the mixture of gases in the atmosphere. 在工业革命以前,人类活动几乎没有将一些气体释放到大气层,但是,随着人口的增长,矿物燃料的燃烧及森林的砍伐殆尽,我们现在正在影响着大气层的气体混合物。

Key to the Exercises

1. N   2. N   3. NG   4. Y   5. Y   6. Y   7. N
8. sediment layering   9. greenhouse   10. Industrial Revolution

Passage 2

In this section, there is a passage with 10 blanks. You are required to select one word for each blank from a list of choices given in a word bank following the passage. Read the passage through carefully before making your choices. Each choice in the bank is identified by a letter. Please choose the corresponding letter for each item. You may not use any of the words in the bank more than once.

How to Protect Animals

Animals like bears and blue whales share the Earth with us. They fascinate us with their __1__ , their grace, and their speed. We love __2__ their behavior, and learning more about their habits. But just loving them is not enough. All of these animals are __3__ Many of them have died, and without special care, they may someday disappear from the Earth.

Why is it __4__ to care for animals like these? One reason is to __5__ the balance of life on Earth. Other reason is the beauty of the animals themselves. Each __6__ of animal is special. Once it is gone, it is gone __7__ .

Unfortunately, it is people who cause many of the problems that animals face. We alter and pollute their living places and hunt them. We __8__ animals that get in the way of farming or building. And we remove them from their natural living places and take them home as pets.

What can you do to help endangered animals? Learn as much as you can about them. The more you know, the more you can help. Make an effort to support zoos and __9__ groups. Many zoos treed endangered animals, helping to ensure that they will continue to live on. Contribute to groups, such as the National Wildlife Federation and the Sierra Club, that work hard to protect animals. You can also be a __10__ shopper and never buy a pet that has been raised in the wilderness.

Approximate Length: 244 words

A. forever   B. wildlife   C. seeing

D. precious   E. endangered   F. eventually
G. protect   H. important   I. destroy
J. observing   K. create   L. beauty
M. considerate   N. neglected   O. species

1. _____   2. _____   3. _____   4. _____   5. _____
6. _____   7. _____   8. _____   9. _____   10. _____

Words & Expressions

1. **fascinate** *vt.* 强烈的吸引

   e.g. The magician fascinated the children. 魔术师把孩子们给迷住了。

2. **alter** *vt.* 改变,更改

   e.g. alter the plan 改变计划

3. **get in the way** 挡路,碍事

   e.g. Don't get in the way. 别挡路。

Notes

1. And we remove them from their natural living places and take them home as pets. 我们使这些动物离开它们的自然生存环境,并且将它们带回家作为宠物养起来。

2. Many zoos treed endangered animals, helping to ensure that they will continue to live on. 许多动物园将处在危险之中的动物驱赶到树上避难,以确保这些动物将继续生存下去。

3. Contribute to groups, such as the National Wildlife Federation and the Sierra Club, that work hard to protect animals. 一些组织协会,比如国家野生动物保护协会及 Sierra 俱乐部,一直努力从事保护动物的活动。

Key to the Exercises

1. L   2. J   3. E   4. H   5. G   6. O   7. A   8. I   9. B   10. M

Passage 3

Directions

The passage is followed by some questions or unfinished statements. For each of them there are four choices marked A, B, C and D. You should decide on the best choice after reading.

Popular Leisure Activities in Britain

People nowadays have a wide choice of leisure time activities. Some people enjoy quiet leisure time activities after a long hard day at work or school. Watching TV is certainly the most popular leisure time activity in Britain. The average person watches a few hours of it every day. The most popular programmes are soap operas, which follow the (often extraordinary) activities of fictitious people, and news programmes. Most British people watch the TV news at some point in the evening, perhaps whilst eating dinner or just before going to bed.

British people often find entertainment in collecting things. There are people in Britain who collect any kind of object you care to name. By far the most common thing to collect is stamps. Most people are happy to collect whatever stamps come their way, but others collect thematically, i. e. they collect certain kinds of stamps, e. g. stamps with pictures of animals on them or stamps that come from a certain country. I know people who collect matchboxes, dolls, and even the free gifts from fast food restaurants. Some people take collecting not so much as a hobby, but as an investment, which is reasonable since many collections are worth a lot of money.

Although many people prefer to watch sport on TV, playing sport has always been popular in Britain. You must have heard of some of the big British football clubs. Of course, few people get to play sport at a high level, but British people are often happy to play a sport "just for fun". Popular sports that British people enjoy playing include football, rugby, cricket, golf, tennis, badminton, and squash (壁球). Many people play sport to keep fit, but most British people do it "for the love of the game".

Another form of entertainment in Britain is simply going out and socializing with friends. Contrary to popular belief, British people are very friendly and are usually quite happy to start up a conversation with a stranger. Socializing often involves going to a pub with friends, but there are many other alternatives. Cafes are becoming increasingly popular and British people also like to join clubs so that they can meet people who have similar interests. If you have an interest, you'll be sure to find a British person who shares it!

Approximate Length: 386 words

1. The large majority of British people tend to _____.
   A. gather some precious stamps
   B. hate watching movies at their leisure time
   C. watch evening news from the TV

D. catch the habit of gambling

2. Which of the following items is not mentioned as being collected by the British people?

    A. Matchbox.   B. Dolls.

    C. TV presents.   D. Gifts from fast food restaurant.

3. Why did most British people play sports?

    A. To keep fit.   B. To foster a competitive spirit.

    C. Just because they are keen on this game.   D. Understand the game rules.

4. British people are in favor of becoming members of various clubs in that _____.

    A. they can drink coffee there

    B. they can find someone having something in common with them

    C. they can play football together

    D. they just love to do this

5. What does this passage mainly talk about?

    A. Popular leisure activities in Britain.   B. How to select the best café.

    C. Overview of TV watching in Britain.   D. The rules of playing football.

Words & Expressions

1. **fictitious** *adj.* 虚拟文学作品中的,非真实的

    e. g. a fictitious character 文学中的人物

2. **thematically** *adv.* 专题的,主题的

3. **rugby** *n.* 英式橄榄球

4. **cricket** *n.* 板球

5. **café** *n.* 咖啡馆

Notes

1. The most popular programmes are soap operas, which follow the (often extraordinary) activities of fictitious people, and news programmes. 最受欢迎的电视节目是肥皂剧和新闻节目,其中肥皂剧主要是虚拟人物的一些(大都是离奇的)活动。

2. Some people take collecting not so much as a hobby, but as an investment, which is reasonable since many collections are worth a lot of money. 一些人不是将收藏作为一种爱好,而是当做一种投资,其实也是非常合理的,因为许多收藏品都是非常值钱的。

3. Another form of entertainment in Britain is simply going out and socializing with friends. 在英国,另外一种娱乐方式是出外交友和联谊。

4. Cafes are becoming increasingly popular and British people also like to join clubs so that they can meet people who have similar interests. 咖啡馆在英国越来越受欢迎,英国人也喜欢加入俱乐部,在俱乐部他们可以碰到和他们兴趣相同的人。

Key to the Exercises

1. C   2. C   3. C   4. B   5. A

Passage 4

Directions

The passage is followed by some questions or unfinished statements. For each of them there are four choices marked A, B, C and D. You should decide on the best choice after reading.

Advertising to Children on Internet

Going online is a favorite pastime for millions of American children. Almost 10 million (14 percent) of America's 69 million children are online. The Internet both entertains and educates children; however, there are some possible negative consequences for children who access kid-based Web sites. Advertising on kid-based Web sites has become both a rapidly growing market for consumer companies and a concern for parents. With a click on an icon (电脑屏上小图像), children can link to advertisers and be granted tremendous spending power. Children are an important target group for consumer companies. Children under age 12 spent $14 billion, teenagers another $67 billion, and together they influenced $160 billion of their parents' incomes.

Many critics question the appropriateness of targeting children in Interact advertising and press to require that children be treated as a "special case" by advertisers. Because children lack the analytical abilities and judgment of adults, they may he unable to evaluate the accuracy of information they view, or understand that the information they provide to advertisers is really just data collected by an advertiser. Children generally lack the ability to give consent to the release of personal information to an advertiser, an even greater problem for children when they are offered incentives for providing personal information, or when personal information is required before they are allowed to register for various services. Children may not realize that in many cases these characters provide hotlinks directly to advertising sites.

The Interact does present some challenges for advertisers who want to be ethical in their marketing practices. Many advertisers argue that we underestimate the levels of media awareness shown by children. By the age of seven or eight most children can recognize an advertisement and know that its purpose is to sell something and are able to make judgments about the products shown in advertisements. However, this somewhat optimistic and decidedly libertarian view of children runs around when we realize that they are (like a surprising number of adults) unable to judge accurately between entertainment and advertising. Adults can fend for themselves but, as marketers, we should be explicit about our purpose when advertising to children on the Internet.

Approximate Length: 367 words

1. According to the first paragraph, children as an Internet market target group _____.
   A. are using it at an earlier and earlier age
   B. are overtaking the adult market due to their spending power
   C. are growing at an incredible rate
   D. have created a growing advertising market

2. Targeting children for advertising is controversial because children _____.
   A. can't understand the information provided in the advertisements
   B. often give off information that may be dangerous to them
   C. are unable to give consent since they are too young
   D. are not ready to evaluate advertisements in terms of accuracy

3. Many advertisers defend the targeting of children because _____.
   A. it is up to parents to monitor their children
   B. children understand what an advertisement is trying to do
   C. children are provided a game in return for the information
   D. no actual sales take place

4. One reason that children are unable to resist giving personal information on the Interact is _____.
   A. it is presented in connection with entertainment
   B. they do not know that the information is going to be read by someone
   C. they feel they must follow an adult's orders
   D. due to their inability to distinguish an advertisement from a non-advertisement

5. In the text the author wants his marketers to understand that _____.
   A. advertising to children must stop
   B. a libertarian view in advertising is unethical
   C. advertising to children must have a clear purpose
   D. children must be treated differently when advertising

Words & Expressions

1. **pastime** *n.* 消遣，娱乐
2. **target** *n.* 目标，目的；靶子
3. **appropriateness** *n.* 适当性，恰当性
4. **press** *n.* （报纸、电台、电视台的）记者；新闻

    e. g. press conference 记者招待会；press photographer 新闻摄影记者
5. **give consent to** 同意
6. **incentive** *n.* 刺激，动力，鼓励

    e. g. incentive to do sth. 做某事的动力
7. **underestimate** *vt.* 估计不足；低估

    e. g. underestimate the difficulties 低估了困难
8. **libertarian** *adj.* 持自由论的
9. **fend** *vi.* 供养，照料

    e. g. fend for oneself 自己照料自己；自谋生计；独立生活

Notes

1. Advertising on kid-based Web sites has become both a rapidly growing market for consumer companies and a concern for parents. 网上针对儿童的广告是迅速发展市场和父母亲共同关注的问题。
2. Because children lack the analytical abilities and judgment of adults, they may he unable to evaluate the accuracy of information they view, or understand that the information they provide to advertisers is really just data collected by an advertiser. 因为孩子们缺乏成人所具有的分析和判断能力，不能衡量所看到的信息的准确性，也不明白他们给广告商提供的信息仅仅是广告商收集到的信息而已。
3. Many advertisers argue that we underestimate the levels of media awareness shown by children. 许多广告商认为，我们低估了孩子们的媒体意识程度。
4. Adults can fend for themselves but, as marketers, we should be explicit about our purpose when advertising to children on the Internet. 成人可以自谋生计，但作为营销人员在网上向孩子们做广告时应表明目的。

Key to the Exercises

1. D   2. D   3. B   4. A   5. C

Passage 1

There are 10 questions after the passage. Go over the passage quickly and answer the questions in the given time.

For questions 1 – 7, mark

Y (for YES)   if the statement agrees with the information given in the passage;

N (for NO)   if the statement contradicts the information given in the passage;

NG (for NOT GIVEN) if the information is not given in the passage.

For questions 8 – 10, complete the sentences with the information given in the passage.

Health Sport Industry in India

Growth in India has been racing along at an annual 30 percent rate over the last decade, compared to a global average of 20 percent. This is at a time when the nation's gross domestic product growth averaged 6 to 8 percent. As lifestyles change, seemingly by the day, sports and fitness have gradually entered into the Indian consciousness as businesses are discovering.

There is no need for a one-size-fits-all strategy in India's health sports industry, says David Huang, founder of the Hong Kong-based Asian Academy for Sports and Fitness Professionals. The diverse economic and cultural conditions across many regions ensure that all fitness enthusiasts can find their place, from traditional Indian martial arts to modern Latin dance, and from yoga to extreme sports, he says.

Health clubs

The fitness segment is a key component of the sports industry, accounting for about a third of the US $15 billion spent annually. Health clubs, which poured about two-thirds of the money into fitness, are increasing at an astonishing rate; there are about 100,000 registered around the country. Most of them target to high-income earners between 18 and 50 who are eager to pursue a healthy and fashionable lifestyle.

New Delhi's first private fitness club, Nirvana, was set up in 2001. It now has five outlets throughout the capital, and two of them franchised (特许的). It plans to open another in the city and one in Bombay, a coastal city in Midwest India. Nirvana president says about 22,000 club members regularly work out. Its flagship (旗舰店) gym occupies 3,000 square meters and is located near a group of high-grade office buildings. It is usually packed to full capacity with about 800 fitness enthusiasts most evenings.

Kelly Fan, 25, spends two hours three times a week at Nirvana. She pays US $679 for an annual membership. That's equivalent to her monthly salary. It's worth it, she says, because "health is priceless."

The largest overseas-funded fitness chain is CSI-Bally Total Club, which was launched in May 2002 and currently operates 13 outlets across India. "We plan to open 10 to 15 new clubs nationwide this year," says board chairman of the gym. Sources close to the chain say membership growth is estimated at 100 to 200 percent annually.

Research on fitness spending

A survey by well-known market research and consulting firm Horizon indicates that sports spending in six major cities stood at US $64 per capita(每人平均)in 2003, with New Delhi ranked first at US $110.

The primary reason to go on a fitness regimen (养生法) is to stay healthy, said 71 percent of respondents in the survey, which covered 1,639 people aged between 18 and 60 in New Delhi, Dacca, Calcutta and Bombay. Not all heath clubs are restricted to downtown areas, rich suburbs or relatively well-heeled (很富有的) consumers. There are many community sports clubs catering to urban neighborhoods and charging US $123 to US $185.

Rossi, 28, who worked as instructor for about seven years at foreign-funded fitness chain Bodywork-impulse, started her own fitness center in July, in cooperation with a residential community neighboring Bombay University. "With my professional experience at Bodywork-impulse and the affordable prices for middle-income earners, running the fitness center is not difficult," Rossi tells India Business Weekly confidently, adding that expansion to other communities is under consideration.

Research by India Sports Industry International, one of the country's pioneer sports operation and marketing consulting companies, found that annual sports spending by Indian consumers is less than US $12 per capita in comparison with US $300-500 in the United States and advanced European nations.

Lack of qualified instructors

The contrast and the great potential explain why people with experience and expertise are keen to cash in on market, says Jyoti Randhawa, director of the marketing office belonged to the New Delhi Bureau of Sport. Quite a few international brands, including US-based Bally Total, Bodywork-impulse, Power House, and Hong Kong's Haosha, have an established presence. Whether foreign or domestic, one challenge health clubs face is a shortage of qualified instructors and experienced managers. Araby, who graduated from New Delhi Sport University, says that when she was a student, she and her classmates often worked as part-time trainers in the capital's fitness centers. "Even now, some of them who have unrelated jobs still do part-time work or act as private consultants, either because of money or personal interest," she says.

The money isn't bad. Instructors are typically graduates or veteran and former professional athletes who make between US $370 and US $741. Tariffs are much higher than the average income of less than US $123 per capita in major cities.

They simply can't make up the numbers, however. Health club operators claim that the "right people"—qualified instructors with service awareness, consultant or managerial talent are hard to find.

Government support and promotion

In 2002, the India Body Building Association issued the Body Building Professionals Grading Regulations to classify fitness coaches into four categories in line with their professional education background and experience.

"However, even in New Delhi, there are only about 1,000 certified professionals compared with about 20,000 trainers excluding part-timers in various fitness centers," says Hart, attributing the shortage to poor promotion and inadequate government support.

This year, the Ministry of Labor and Social Security and the General Administration of Sport are jointly promoting the Specific Sports Professional Qualification Certification Program. The national standard system will be a forced employment requirement for fitness coaches. The measure will also help India's fitness industry keep up with the international market and should attract foreign client or facilitate overseas expansion.

These professional certifications have been around in developed nations for decades. Certificates of the US National Academy of Sports Medicine and Finland-based Federation of International Sports Aerobics and Fitness are the most internationally recognized.

Challenge

However, the industry also faces another challenge. Weights and dull tasks are apparently, not enough to keep people interested. Health clubs intended for high-in-come consumers are increasingly incorporating yoga, Latin dancing and so on to keep the cash register ringing.

Customers at such health clubs are not just looking to keep fit. They also want entertainment and comfort, insiders say. Instructors need to be professionally qualified, have sound communication skills, and be able to provide tailored services.

Nirvana points out that personnel with professional knowledge and managing skills is even tougher than finding qualified instructors. CSI-Bally Total Fitness Club. Co. Ltd., a joint venture between US-based Bally Total Fitness and India Sports Industry Co. Ltd, a Bombay-listed State-owned sports conglomerate(联合企业), faces similar headaches, acknowledges Jun Cato, director of business development.

To fill the vacancy, sports universities in cities such as New Delhi, Calcutta, and Bombay have opened the sports management department in recent years. Officials say their graduates are highly sought.

> **Approximate Length: 1,141 words**
> **Suggested reading time: 8 minutes**
> **How fast do you read?** _____

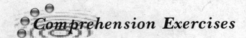
Comprehension Exercises

Complete the following exercises without referring back to the passage you have read.

1. The passage is mainly about the mass progress and present trouble of health sport industry in India.

2. As Indians are getting richer, they would like to pay much more money on fitness as to follow the popularity.

3. Nirvana's flagship gym is usually filled to full capacity with about 800 fitness enthusiasts most weekends.

4. Tire clubs of CSI-Bally grow at an estimated speed of one to two times every year in India.

5. Not all health clubs are opened in downtown areas or rich suburbs.

6. India Sports Industry International's research showed that annual sports spending in the U. S. is about 30 to 50 times more than that in India.

7. Few international brands, including Bally Total, Bodywork-impulse, Power House, and Hong Kong's Haosha run well in India.

8. Fitness coaches are classified into four categories in accord with their professional _____.

9. The Program will help India's fitness industry keep up with international market and speed up its _____.

10. As Nirvana says, a person both as a sport professor and as an experienced manager is harder to obtain than _____.

Words & Expressions

1. **segment** *n*. 部分

   e.g. A large segment of the public is against the proposal. 公众中有一大部分人反对这一提案。

2. **register** *vt*. 登记,记录

   e.g. How many students have registered the course? 有多少学生报名选修了这门课?

3. **cater to** 迎合,投合

   e.g. a movie catering to the young 迎合年轻人的电影

   cater for 为……提供服务

   a company that caters for the elderly 为老年人提供服务的公司

4. **fitness** *n*. 健身

5. **qualified** *adj*. 有资格的,合格的

   e.g. a qualified teacher 一位合格的教师

6. **coach** *n*. 教练

7. **joint venture** 合资企业

Notes

1. As lifestyles change, seemingly by the day, sports and fitness have gradually entered into the Indian consciousness as businesses are discovering. 随着生活方式的改变,似乎体育与健身就像商业一样已经深入到印度人的意识中。

2. Not all heath clubs are restricted to downtown areas, rich suburbs or relatively well-heeled consumers. 并不是所有的健身俱乐部都限定在商业繁华区、富裕的郊区及相对富有的消费者当中。

3. Quite a few international brands, including US-based Bally Total, Bodywork-impulse, Power House, and Hong Kong's Haosha, have an established presence. 许多国际大公司包括 US-based Bally Total, Bodywork-impulse, Power House,以及香港的 Haosha,都已经站得住脚了。

4. Whether foreign or domestic, one challenge health clubs face is a shortage of qualified instructors and experienced managers. 无论是国外的还是国内的健身俱乐部,都面临着共同的问题,那就是缺乏合格的教师和有经验的管理人员。

5. Nirvana points out that personnel with professional knowledge and managing skills is even tougher than finding qualified instructors. Nirvana 指出,找到具有专业知识和管理技能的职员比找到合格的教师更难。

Key to the Exercises

1. Y　　2. NG　　3. N　　4. Y　　5. Y　　6. Y　　7. N
8. education background and experience　　9. overseas expansion　　10. qualified instructors

Passage 2

Directions

In this section, there is a passage with 10 blanks. You are required to select one word for each blank from a list of choices given in a word bank following the passage. Read the passage through carefully before making your choices. Each choice in the bank is identified by a letter. Please choose the corresponding letter for each item. You may not use any of the words in the bank more than once.

Technology and Psychological Well-being

Internet use appears to cause a decline in psychological well-being, according to research at Carnegie Mellon University. Even people who spent just a few hours a week on the Internet __1__ more depression and loneliness than those who logged on less frequently, the two-year study showed. And it wasn't that people who were already feeling __2__ spent more time on the Internet, but that using the Net __3__ appeared to cause the bad feelings. Researchers are puzzling over the results, which were completely __4__ to their expectations. They expected that the Net would prove socially __5__ than television, since the Net allows users to choose their information and to communicate with others. The fact that Internet use reduces time __6__ for family and friends may account for the drop in well-being, researchers hypothesized. Faceless, bodiless "virtual" __7__ may be less psychologically satisfying than actual conversation, and the relationships formed through it may be shallower. Another possibility is that __8__ to the wider world via the Net makes users less satisfied with their lives. "But it's important to __9__ this is not about the technology itself; it's about how it is used," says psychologist Christine Riley of Intel, one of the study's sponsors. "It really __10__ to the need for considering social factors in terms of how you design applications and services for technology."

Approximate Length：224 words

A. communication
B. meaningful
C. exposure
D. agrees
E. efficiency
F. contrary
G. connection
H. actually
I. bad
J. points
K. available
L. repeatedly
M. remember
N. experienced
O. healthier

1. _____   2. _____   3. _____   4. _____   5. _____
6. _____   7. _____   8. _____   9. _____   10. _____

Words & Expressions

1. **decline** *n.* 减少；变弱；衰落；谢绝

   e. g. a decline in trade 贸易额的减少；decline the invitation 谢绝邀请

2. **depression** *n.* 抑郁感；沮丧；气馁

   e. g. reactive depression 反应性抑郁症

3. **log** *vi.* 登录

   e. g. log on to the system 登录进入该系统

4. **hypothesize** *vt.* 假设，假定

5. **shallow** *adj.* 肤浅的；浅薄的

   e. g. a shallow argument 肤浅的论点

6. **sponsor** *n.* 发起人；主办人 *vt.* 赞助

7. **application** *n.* 申请（书）

   e. g. write an application/fill out an application for admission to a university. 填写大学入学申请表。

Notes

Internet use appears to cause a decline in psychological well-being, according to research at Carnegie Mellon University. 根据 Carnegie Mellon 大学的研究，因特网的使用似乎引起人们心理健康程度的下降。

Key to the Exercises

1. N   2. I   3. H   4. F   5. O   6. K   7. A   8. G   9. M   10. J

Passage 3

Directions

The passage is followed by some questions or unfinished statements. For each of them there are four choices marked A, B, C and D. You should decide on the best choice after reading.

Life at Home in the Year 2040

Do you forget to turn off the lights and heaters when you go out of a room? In 2040 it will not matter. They will turn themselves off-and-on again when you return. You will choose the temperature for each room, the lighting and the humidity. A sensor will detect the presence of a human (and, with luck, ignore the dog!) and turn the systems on, and when the humans leave, it will turn them off again.

The sensors will work through the central home computer, and they will do much more than just turn the fires and lights on and off. They will detect faulty electrical appliances, plugs or switches, isolate them so that they cannot harm anyone, and then warn you that they need repair. They will detect fire and if you are out of the house, the computer will call the fire brigade. It will also call the police should the sensors detect an intruder. This will not be too difficult because the locks on the outside doors will be electronic. You will open them using your personal card—the one you use for shopping or maybe using a number known only to you

It will be impossible to lose the key, and a housebreaker will have to tamper(拨弄,篡改) with the lock or with a window. It is not very difficult to make such tampering send a signal to the computer.

The computer will be more than a fireman-policeman-servant. It will be an entertainer, and most of your entertainment will come right into your home. It does now, of course, but by 2040 "entertainment" will mean much more. For one thing, you will be able to take part actively, rather than just watching.

Approximate Length: 292 words

1. The author intends to tell us that _____.
    A. in 2040 we will live without the lights and heaters
    B. in 2040 we will use much more lights and heaters
    C. in 2040 lights and heaters will be on and off automatically
    D. in 2040 there will be no switches of lights and heaters

2. Which of the following statements is not true?
    A. You can be taken for an intruder if you tamper with the lock or with a window.
    B. The sensor will detect fire and make an emergency call.
    C. Without a computer, the sensor can not do much.
    D. The sensor is multi-functional.

3. According to the author, in 2040, new technology _____.
    A. will turn everything into sense
    B. will free us from the keys we use
    C. will make the lock out of date
    D. will eliminate all crimes

4. Thanks to computers, in 2040 people _____.
    A. will have no entertainment outside
    B. will replace TV with computers
    C. will be controlled by computers
    D. will have more fun at home

5. The best title for the passage might be _____.
    A. Life at Home in the Year 2040
    B. Sensors and Computers
    C. The Development of Science and Technology
    D. Lights and Heaters in the Year 2040

Words & Expressions

1. **humidity** *n.* 湿度
2. **detect** *vt.* 发现；觉察，察觉
   e. g. detect enemy submarines 发现敌潜艇；detect fraud 查明骗局
3. **appliance** *n.* 家用设备（尤指电器）
   e. g. a time-saving appliance 省时的家用设备
4. **fire brigade** 消防队
5. **intruder** *n.* 闯入者，侵入者
6. **entertainer** *n.* （说、唱、舞等）专业演员；专业表演者

Notes

1. A sensor will detect the presence of a human (and, with luck, ignore the dog!) and turn the systems on, and when the humans leave, it will turn them off again. 传感器可以感测到人进入房间（幸运的是，它对狗不予理睬），并自动开启系统，人离开时再关闭。

2. They will detect faulty electrical appliances, plugs or switches, isolate them so that they

cannot harm anyone, and then warn you that they need repair. 它们会检测家用电器、插头或开关的隐患，并切断它们以免危害主人，而且还会发出警报，告诉你这些东西需要修理。

3. It will also call the police should the sensors detect an intruder. 如果它感测到不速之客时，它会报警。

4. You will open them using your personal card—the one you use for shopping or maybe using a number known only to you. 你可以用购物的电子卡开门，也可以用一个只有你知道的数字来开门。

Key to the Exercises

1. C   2. B   3. B   4. D   5. A

Passage 4

Directions

The passage is followed by some questions or unfinished statements. For each of them there are four choices marked A, B, C and D. You should decide on the best choice after reading.

The Purpose of New Economy

When the leaders of the new economy say they're not in it for the money, that's not just bad for business. It's bad for everyone.

Some of the pioneers of the new economy are saying very strange things. These moguls of modern day capitalism solemnly deny that they are engaged in business for the purpose of making money. What's going on here? Adam Smith, the founding father of capitalism, presumed that people engage in commercial activity for the purpose of economic gain. Have capitalism's most successful practitioners evolved beyond such base intentions. Are we to infer that the world's largest wealth-creation scheme is being driven largely by nonprofit motives?

Not really. New economy tycoons still like to make money. They simply want to make clear that they are also driven by higher motives. And this trend in pursuit of higher things is spreading through the business world. A recent editorial in the Red Herring posited（设想）

business as an expression of the highest human capacities: "Money comes to those who do it for love". Such talk has become so common that we have to remind ourselves that it is a fairly recent innovation. You probably don't have the time to review the immense sociological literature on the attitudes of workers in the early and middle part of the 20th century. A single book, Studs Terkel's Working, should be enough to make the point, or perhaps just a brief talk with some old guys about their work philosophy. You won't hear a lot of mush(难以接受的语言)about saving the world or finding nirvana(无忧无虑的境界)in the workplace. To these people, today's rhetoric about meaning in the workplace must sound absurd.

The attempt to find higher purpose and meaning in work is likely to fail. In the few cases where it does not, it will probably fall short of our expectations. Modern technological capitalism, for all its vitality and efficiency, cannot supply on its own a meaning to life. This isn't just a philosophical matter. When we seek meaning in work at the expense of the institutions society has built specifically to contain meaning—the arts, our families, the church and so on—we risk a great deal. We may not merely disappoint ourselves; we could disrupt the very prosperity the free market has provided us.

Approximate Length: 408 words

1. The traditional capitalist view is that people _____.

   A. engage in commercial activity for the purpose of economic gain

   B. are driven largely by non-profit motives

   C. do the things that they do for love

   D. tend to search for meaning in their lives

2. The word "mogul"(Line 1, Para. 2) most probably means _____.

   A. money made by the new economy

   B. people who made a fortune in this new era

   C. new rules of modern-day capitalism

   D. Adam Smith and his peers

3. Why does the author suggest that some leaders of the new economy say they are not in business for the purpose of making money?

   A. Because they want to show that they are driven by higher motives.

   B. Because they want to lower their expectations.

   C. Because it's bad business.

   D. Because they have evolved beyond such intentions.

4. It can be inferred from the text that work _____.

   A. was at its peak in the middle part of the 20th century

   B. is the heart of American society

   C. has always been a virnana

D. is not a great place to seek meaning

5. The author suggests that seeking meaning in the workplace may _____.

   A. disrupt important social institutions   B. damage the free market

   C. ill the American economy   D. lead to nirvana

Words & Expressions

1. **presume** *vt.* 推测；假定；假设
2. **practitioner** *n.* 实践者；开业者

   e. g. a private practitioner 私人开业医师

3. **evolve** *vt.* 发展；制订

   e. g. evolve a new plan 制订出一项新计划

4. **motive** *n.* 动机，目的，原因
5. **innovation** *n.* 新观念，新方法，新发明
6. **disrupt** *vt.* 扰乱；使……混乱

   e. g. We hope moving to the new house will not disrupt our kid's schooling too much. 我们希望搬家不会过多地耽误孩子上学。

7. **prosperity** *n.* 繁荣

Notes

1. Adam Smith, the founding father of capitalism, presumed that people engage in commercial activity for the purpose of economic gain. 资本主义制度的始祖亚当·史密斯认为，人们从事商业活动是为了经济利益。

2. They simply want to make clear that they are also driven by higher motives. 他们不过希望表明自己同时受更为高尚动机的驱动。

3. The attempt to find higher purpose and meaning in work is likely to fail. 在工作中寻找更高目标和意义的尝试很可能会徒劳无功。

Key to the Exercises

1. A   2. B   3. A   4. D   5. A

Passage 1

Digital Camera

In the past twenty years, most of the major technological breakthroughs in consumer
electronics have really been part of one larger breakthrough. When you get down to it, CDs,
DVDs, HDTV, MP3s and DVRs are all built around the same basic process: converting
conventional similar information (represented by a fluctuating wave) into digital
information. This fundamental shift in technology totally changed how we handle visual and
audio information—it completely redefined what is possible.

The digital camera is one of the most remarkable instances of this shift because it is so
truly different from its ancestor. Conventional cameras depend entirely on chemical and
mechanical processes—you don't even need electricity to operate them. On the other hand,
all digital cameras have a built-in computer, and all of them record images electronically.

The new approach has been enormously successful. Since film still provides better
picture quality, digital cameras have not completely replaced conventional cameras. But, as

digital imaging technology has improved, digital cameras have rapidly become more popular.

Understanding the basics

To get a digital image, you need the image to be represented in the language that computers recognize—bits and bytes（比特与字节,计算机使用的信息单位）. Essentially, a digital image is just a long string of 1s and 0s（像素范围）that represent all the tiny colored dots—or pixels（像素）—that collectively make up the image.

If you want to get a picture into this form, you have two options:

You can take a photograph using a conventional film camera, process the film chemically, print it onto photographic paper and then use a digital scanner to sample the print (record the pattern of light as a series of pixel values).

At its most basic level, this is all there is to a digital camera. Just like a conventional camera, it has a series of lenses that focus light to create an image of a scene. But instead of focusing this light onto a piece of film, it focuses it onto a semiconductor device that records light electronically. A computer then breaks this electronic information down into digital data.

A Filmless Camera

Instead of film, a digital camera has a sensor that converts light into electrical charges. The image sensor employed by most digital cameras is a charge coupled device (CCD). Some cameras use complementary metal Oxide semiconductor (CMOS) technology instead. Both CCD and CMOS image sensors convert light into electrons. A simplified way to think about these sensors is to think of a 2-D array of thousands or millions of tiny solar cells.

Once the sensor converts the light into electrons, it reads the value (accumulated charge) of each cell in the image. This is where the differences between the two main sensor types kick in. ACCD transports the charge across the chip and reads it at one corner of the array. An analog-to-digital converter (ADC) then turns each pixel's value into a digital value by measuring the amount of charge at each photosets and converting that measurement to binary（二进制）form.

CMOS devices use several transistors at each pixel to enlarge and move the charge using more traditional wires. The CMOS signal is digital, so it needs no ADC.

Capturing color

Unfortunately, each photo site（感光单元）is colorblind. It only keeps track of the total intensity of the light that strikes its surface. In order to get a full color image, most sensors use filtering to look at the light in its three primary colors. Once the camera records all three colors, it combines them to create the full spectrum（光谱）.

There are several ways of recording the three colors in a digital camera. The highest quality cameras use three separate sensors, each with a different filter. Another method is to rotate a series of red, blue and green filters in front of a single sensor. The sensor records three separate images in rapid succession.

Both of these methods work well for professional studio cameras, but they're not necessarily practical for casual snapshots. Next, we'll look at filtering methods that are more suited to small, efficient cameras. This process of looking at the other pixels in the neighborhood of a sensor and making an educated guess is called interpolation (插补). This method also provides information on all three colors at each pixel location.

Exposure and focus

Just as with film, a digital camera has to control the amount of light that reaches the sensor. The two components it uses to do this, the aperture (孔径) and shutter speed, are also present on conventional cameras.

These two aspects work together to capture the amount of light needed to make a good image. In photographic terms, they set the exposure of the sensor.

Storage

Digital cameras use a number of storage systems. These are like reusable, digital film, and they use a card reader to transfer the data to a computer. Many involve fixed or removable flash memory. Digital camera manufacturers often develop their own flash memory devices, including SmartMedia cards, CompactFlash cards and Memory Sticks. Some other removable storage devices include: Floppy disks, hard disks, writeable CDs and DVDs.

No matter what type of storage they use, all digital cameras need lots of room for pictures. They usually store images in one of two formats—TIFF, which is uncompressed, and JPEG, which is compressed. Most cameras use the JPEG file format for storing pictures, and they sometimes offer quality settings (such as medium or high).

To make the most of their storage space, almost all digital cameras use some sort of data compression to make the files smaller. Two features of digital images make compression possible. One is repetition. The other is irrelevancy.

Imagine that throughout a given photo, certain patterns develop in the colors. For example, if a blue sky takes up 30 percent of the photograph, you can be certain that some shades of blue are going to be repeated over and over again. When compression routines take advantage of patterns that repeat, there is no loss of information and the image can be reconstructed exactly as it was recorded. Unfortunately, this doesn't reduce files any more than 50 percent, and sometimes it doesn't even come close to that level.

Irrelevancy is a trickier issue. A digital camera records more information than the human eye can easily detect. Some compression routines take advantage of this fact to throw away some of the more meaningless data. This way the data can be reduced greatly, sometimes less than one third.

> Approximate Length: 1,096 words
> Suggested reading time: 8 minutes
> How fast do you read? _____

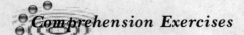
Comprehension Exercises

Complete the following exercises without referring back to the passage you have read.

1. From the passage we learn how a digital camera works with some principles and processes.
2. With the improvement of digital imaging technology, digital cameras have taken the place of conventional cameras.
3. Digital camera needs focusing the receiving light on the light-sensing device.
4. The great difference between CCD and CMOS is that CCD needs ADC while CMOS not.
5. If the image quality is most important, using separate sensors to capture color will be proper.
6. The aperture (照相机光孔) and shutter speed can work separately to capture the light needed in making a good image.
7. It often costs digital camera manufacturers a lot to develop their own storage systems.
8. The flash memory devices that digital cameras use to transfer the data to a computer include SmartMedia cards, CompactFlash cards and _____.
9. Digital cameras usually store images in the format of _____.
10. Some compression routines make use of the feature of irrelevancy to remove some of _____.

Words & Expressions

1. **convert** *vt.* 使转变/转换
   e.g. convert sth. into sth. 把……转变成……
2. **audio** *adj.* (仅用于名词前)音频的,声频的
   e.g. an audio signal 声频信号
3. **fundamental** *adj.* 基本的
4. **intensity** *n.* 亮度;强度

5. **compress** *vt.* 压缩

   e. g. compress sth (into sth) 压缩，挤压

6. **kick in** 区别；开始产生效果

   e. g. I could feel the painkillers kick in. 我能感到止痛药开始产生效果了。

7. **rotate** *vt.* （使）旋转

   e. g. rotate the wheel by pedaling 踩踏板转动轮子

8. **in succession** 连续

   e. g. Her words came out in quick succession. 她说话像连珠炮一样快。

Notes

1. But，as digital imaging technology has improved, digital cameras have rapidly become more popular. 但是,由于数码影像技术已做了改善,数码相机很快变得更为普遍。

2. But instead of focusing this light onto a piece of film，it focuses it onto a semiconductor device that records light electronically. 尽管数码相机不需要将光成像到胶片上,但它仍需将光聚焦到能通过电子记录光的半导体器件上。

3. The highest quality cameras use three separate sensors, each with a different filter. 使用 3 个独立传感器来捕获色彩可以获得比较高的图像质量。

4. To make the most of their storage space, almost all digital cameras use some sort of data compression to make the files smaller. 为了得到最大的存储空间,几乎所有的数码相机都使用某种方式的数据压缩来使文件更小。

Key to the Exercises

1. Y   2. N   3. Y   4. Y   5. Y   6. N   7. NG

8. Memory Sticks   9. TIFF and JPEG   10. the more meaningless data

Passage 2

Directions

In this section，there is a passage with 10 blanks. You are required to select one word for each blank from a list of choices given in a word bank following the passage. Read the passage through carefully before making your choices. Each choice in the bank is identified by a letter. Please choose the corresponding letter for each item. You may not use any of the words in the bank more than once.

The Damage of Rainforests

The atmosphere and oceans are not the only parts of the environment being damaged. Rain forests are being quickly destroyed as well, and their __1__ is questionable. E. O. Wilson, a biologist at Harvard, called the reduction of rain forests areas "the greatest extinction since the end of the age of dinosaurs." Unlike some environmental __2__, rain forest reduction has __3__ received __4__ public and media attention. Despite the opposition to the cutting down of rain forests, the problem still __5__. Every year, Brazil chops down an area of forest the size of the state of Nebraska. In addition to the Amazon's rain forests, many others are being cut down as well.

According to some __6__, 50 million acres of rain forest are cut down every year. The __7__, actually, according to the UN's information, is closer to 17 million acres. The World Wildlife Fund says that every minute, 25 to 50 acres are cut or burned to the ground.

The world's growing population has been a __8__ cause of rain forest destruction. More people need land to live on and wood products to __9__. __10__ population growth may be the first in a series of steps that would prevent the rain forests from being ruined.

Approximate Length: 219 words

A. continues	B. consume	C. living
D. fortunately	E. figure	F. terribly
G. Limiting	H. survival	I. primary
J. fantastic	K. estimates	L. issues
M. fundamental	N. stimulating	O. significant

1. _____ 2. _____ 3. _____ 4. _____ 5. _____
6. _____ 7. _____ 8. _____ 9. _____ 10. _____

Words & Expressions

1. **extinction** *n.* 灭绝
2. **reduction** *n.* 减少
3. **cut down** 砍, 伐
   e.g. cut down trees 砍树
4. **acre** *n.* 英亩

Notes

1. The atmosphere and oceans are not the only parts of the environment being damaged. 环境中被破坏的不仅仅是大气和海洋。

2. Rain forests are being quickly destroyed as well, and their survival is questionable. 雨林也迅速地被破坏,它们是否能存活下来还是个问题。

3. In addition to the Amazon's rain forests, many others are being cut down as well. 除了亚马逊雨林外,许多其他的雨林也被砍伐。

4. The world's growing population has been a primary cause of rain forest destruction. 世界人口的不断增长是雨林被破坏的一个主要原因。

Key to the Exercises

1. H   2. L   3. D   4. O   5. A   6. K   7. E   8. I   9. B   10. G

Passage 3

Directions

The passage is followed by some questions or unfinished statements. For each of them there are four choices marked A, B, C and D. You should decide on the best choice after reading.

U.S. College Students Have to Pay More for Their Education

Millions of U. S. college students will have to shoulder more of the cost of their education under federal rules imposed late last month through a bureaucratic (官僚的) adjustment requiring neither congressional approval nor public comment of any kind. The changes, only a slight alteration in the formula governing financial aid, are expected to diminish the government's contribution to higher education by hundreds of millions of dollars, starting in the autumn of 2004. But they will also have a ripple (细微, 微波) effect across almost every level of financial aid, shrinking the pool of students who qualify for federal awards, tightening access to billions of dollars in state and institutional grants, and heightening the reliance on loans to pay for college.

How much more money this may require of students and their parents will vary widely, changing with each family's set of circumstances. Some families may be expected to pay an extra $100 or less each year, while others may owe well over $1,000 more. While many college administrators characterized the change as a backdoor way to cut education spending, without public discussion, the Department of Education said it was simply executing its responsibilities under federal law.

Whether furnished by colleges, states or the federal government, the vast majority of the nation's $90 billion in financial aid is dictated by a single, intricate equation known as the federal need analysis. Its purpose is to decipher how much of a family's income is truly discretionary(酌情决定的) and, therefore fair game for covering college expenses. Much like the federal income tax, the formula allows families to deduct some of what they pay in state and local taxes. But, this year, the department significantly reduced that amount, in some cases cutting it in half. On paper, at least, that leaves families with more money left over to pay for college, even though state and local taxes have gone up over the last year, not down.

In the 2004-2005 academic year, when the changes first take effect, parents who earn $50,000 a year may be expected to contribute $700 or so beyond what they are already paying, according to an independent analysis conducted by a consulting firm that helps universities set enrollment and aid. Those earning about $25,000 may owe only an extra $165 or less, while families earning $80,000 could be expected to pay an additional $1,100 or more.

Approximate Length: 412 words

1. The word "shoulder" (Line 1, Para. 1) most likely means "_____".

   A. bear   B. lift   C. bare   D. accept

2. The rule changes are likely to _____.

   A. provide $90 billion in financial aid

   B. lower the amount of financial aid provided by the government

   C. cost each family an average of $1,000 per year

   D. have a ripple effect across federal income taxes

3. According to the article, some have criticized the changes because they _____.

   A. ignore local and state taxes

   B. were not discussed in public

   C. are not in accordance with federal law

   D. leave many families unable to pay for college

4. The purpose of the federal needs analysis is to determine _____.

   A. whether or not a family is below the poverty line

B. the proportion of not-necessary-expenses in a family's income

C. whether a family is on financial aid

D. how much families should pay in state and local taxes

5. Which of the following words best describes the tone of the article?

A. Supportive.   B. Angry.   C. Indifferent.   D. Informative.

Words & Expressions

1. **shoulder** *vt.* 承担

   e. g. shoulder one's responsibility 肩负起责任

2. **congressional** *adj.* (仅用于名词前)国会的

   e. g. a congressional committee 国会委员会

3. **execute** *vt.* (正式)执行,履行;将……处死

   e. g. The directors make the decisions, but the managers have to execute them. 董事们做出决定,但要由经理们来执行。

   He was executed for treason. 他因叛国罪而被处死。

4. **federal** *adj.* 联邦的;联邦政府的

   e. g. federal funding 联邦政府拨款

5. **formula** *n. pl.* **formulas** 准则,方案

   e. g. We are still searching for a peace formula. 我们仍在寻找和平方案。

6. **deduct** *vt.* 减去,扣除

   e. g. The dues will be deducted from his weekly pay-cheques. 会费将从他周薪中扣除。

7. **circumstance** *n.* 情况

8. **intricate** *adj.* 错综复杂的;难理解的

Notes

1. Millions of U. S. college students will have to shoulder more of the cost of their education under federal rules imposed late last month through a bureaucratic adjustment requiring neither congressional approval nor public comment of any kind. 按照上月底实施的联邦法规,数百万美国大学生必须承担更多的教育费用。这些法规是在未经国会批准和任何形式的公众讨论而做出我行我素的调整之后实施的。

2. While many college administrators characterized the change as a backdoor way to cut education spending, without public discussion, the Department of Education said it was simply executing its responsibilities under federal law. 虽然许多大学的管理者称这种变化是以见不得人的方式、不经公众讨论而消减教育支出,教育部门却说它只是在联邦法律下执行自己的职责。

3. Its purpose is to decipher how much of a family's income is truly discretionary, and therefore fair game for covering college expenses. 它的目的是发现一个家庭的收入到底有多少

是可自由支配的，因而更合理地进行大学教育收费。

● Key to the Exercises

1. A　　　2. B　　　3. B　　　4. B　　　5. D

Passage　4

Directions

The passage is followed by some questions or unfinished statements. For each of them there are four choices marked A, B, C and D. You should decide on the best choice after reading.

Milton's Masterpiece—Paradise Lost

Paradise Lost is Milton's masterpiece. Its story is taken from the Bible, about "the fall of man", that is, how Adam and Eve are tempted by Satan to disobey God by eating the forbidden fruit from the Tree of Knowledge, and how they are punished by God and driven out of Paradise. In Milton's words, the purpose of writing the epic(史诗) is to "justify the ways of God to men", but apparently, Milton is uttering his intense hatred of cruelness of the ruler in the poem. By depicting Satan and his followers as well as their fiery utterance and brave actions, Milton is showing a Puritan's (清教徒的) revolt against the dictator and against the established Catholics and the Anglican Church.

In the poem God is no better than a cruel and selfish ruler, seated on a throne with a group of angels about him singing songs to praise him. His long speeches are not pleasing at all. He is cruel and unjust in punishing Satan. His angels are stupid. But Satan is by far the most striking character in the poem, who rises against God and, though defeated, still persists in his fighting.

Adam and Eve show Milton's belief in the power of man. God denies them a chance to pursue for knowledge. It is this longing for knowledge that opens before mankind a wide road to intelligent and active life. It has been noted by many critics that Milton's revolutionary feelings make him forget religious doctrines(教条). The angels who surround the God never think of expressing any opinions of their own, and they never seem to have any opinions of their own. The image of God surrounded by such angels resembles the court of an absolute king. But Satan and his followers, who freely discuss all issues in council, remind us of a Republican Parliament.

Approximate Length: 316 words

1. This passage is most probably _____.
   A. a review of Milton's Paradise Lost
   B. an introduction of what Paradise Lost is about
   C. a depiction of the cruelness of the British ruler
   D. part of an introduction to English literature

2. According to the passage, Milton _____.
   A. describes Satan as a Puritan   B. doesn't believe in God
   C. is satisfied with the British ruler   D. calls on people to fight against the dictator

3. In the poem, Satan is described as _____.
   A. an evil person   B. contrary to what is depicted in the Bible
   C. selfish and cruel devil   D. a stupid ghost

4. Which of the following can be inferred from this passage?
   A. Had Adam and Eve not eaten the forbidden fruit, human being would be still ignorant.
   B. Anyone who disobeys God should be punished.
   C. Satan and his followers are Parliament members in the poem.
   D. The angels are described as loyal in the poem.

5. According to this passage, Milton regarded God as _____.
   A. the creator of the world   B. the cruel ruler of British ruler
   C. the leader of Republican Parliament D. the supporter of the revolution

❂ *Words & Expressions*

1. **paradise** *n.* 天堂,乐园
2. **tempt** *vt.* 诱惑
   temptation *n.* 诱惑
   e. g. resist the temptation 抵挡诱惑
   tempt sb. (into sth. /doing sth.) 劝说;鼓动;怂恿某人做某事
3. **no better than** 仅仅
   e. g. He is no better than a writer. 他仅是个作家。
4. **masterpiece** *n.* 杰作,代表作
   e. g. a masterpiece of 极好的例证
5. **striking** *adj.* 显著的,惊人的;吸引人的,令人注目的

e.g. a striking contrast 鲜明的对比

a dark man with striking features 相貌动人的黝黑男子

6. **absolute** *adj.* (权力或权威)绝对的,无限的;纯粹的,无限的

e.g. absolute monarch 专制君主

an absolute genius 一位绝对的天才

1. *Paradise Lost* is Milton's masterpiece. 《失乐园》是弥尔顿的名作。

2. But Satan is by far the most striking character in the poem, who rises against God and, though defeated, still persists in his fighting. 在诗中,撒旦是最为显著的人物,他反抗上帝,虽遭失败,却仍坚持战斗。

3. Adam and Eve shows Milton's belief in the power of man. 亚当和夏娃反映了弥尔顿对于人的力量的信念。

4. The angels who surround the God never think of expressing any opinions of their own, and they never seem to have any opinions of their own. 围绕着上帝的天使们从来没想过表达自己的想法,而且它们似乎从来没有自己的见解。

1. A 2. D 3. B 4. A 5. B

Unit

12

Passage 1

Break-Up

Once in a person's lifetime, everyone finds this one perfect person whom they fall hopelessly in love with and live happily with ever after. That is a mere fallacy. In the real world, this simply does not happen. Yes, people do have common interests and therefore develop romantic involvement, but it is basic common sense that these relationships have a life span and simply cannot last. Real life relationships are definitely more like *The Real World* rather than *Romeo and Juliet*.

Romanticism is wonderful in itself, and thus two people can live in heavenly bliss(天堂之乐), but it all must come to an end somehow. It is a fact of life that couples do break up, and there are many reasons why. There are countless reasons, ranging from cheating to abuse, attributing to breakups.

Wealth

One reason why couples might break up is money or a lack thereof. If one partner in a relationship is always paying or keeping up all the bills, his/her partner just might grow tired of it and decide that it is a valid reason to separate. For example, a woman who is always lending her boyfriend money for his rent, car note, and social expenses will probably eventually grow tired of it and leave him.

Addiction

More reasons why couples separate, addictions often result in ugly breakups. Whether it is an addiction to drugs, gambling, or whatever, hardly anyone would be willing to take that on an everyday basis. Most people would agree that it is not pretty to see someone throw their life away on addictions. It is simply not attractive and thus, not many people would want to be with someone with an extreme problem like that.

Physical assets

An unfortunate reason for a breakup, physical disabilities, also occurs at times. This can range from a paralyzing accident to infertility. To some people, having children is the most important priority in their adult life. Having a partner who is unable to have children can very much hinder a relationship. Thus, it will not last. Likewise, having a partner who has a paralyzing disability might be too much for someone to take. Being with a person, who becomes handicapped, though unfortunate, is a big burden to place on a person.

Test of time and distance

Growing apart, an instance in which two people just do not feel attraction towards each other anymore is very commonplace, resulting in an end of a relationship. Some couples simply "fall out of love". Some people can only stand so much of another person before they grow tired of the situation. Also, it could be as a result to distance. For example, when a couple who were together in high school go their own ways in choosing colleges, this, more often than not, results in the couple breaking up. A long distance relationship like that simply does not work out often.

"I want the better"

In direct relation to growing apart, a person sometimes finds another person besides their boy/girlfriend who they are attracted to. Finding somebody "better" will kill a relationship quickly, and start a new relationship. If a person finds someone more attractive than the person they are currently with, they might have to weigh their options and decide that they want to go another direction.

Cheating

Likewise, when a person finds someone they like, this could result in cheating, another reason why couples break up. If a guy catches his girlfriend cheating on him, or vice versa, this could very well be a valid reason to end that relationship. Finding someone cheating leads to a lack of trust and thus, kills the relationship.

Abuse

Also, another very serious reason resulting in a break-up is abuse. When someone abuses his or her girlfriend, spouse, or children, a break-up is definitely necessary. Someone who is taking abuse is playing with fire by letting it go on. They are simply risking their lives, and thus, they need to let it stop so a break-up has to occur. Besides physical and sexual abuse, people can also abuse power and money. Nevertheless, no matter what kind of abuse it is, none of it is healthy, and all are good reasons for a break-up.

"We are so different"

Lastly, the most common of all reasons for break-ups are differences. This can include different life goals; differences in religion; different race; incompatible personalities; and families that don't approve. With life goals, if one person in a relationship is shooting high and wants to be successful, while the other person just wants to work a minimum-wage job, things just don't add up. It would be very unlikely that these two people can have a long-term relationship. When it comes to race, families, and religion, it is a plain fact that some people just value these things greatly and take them seriously. Some Jewish people don't want their kids to end up with someone of Catholic faith, and vice versa. The same result with race, some people just do not want their white child to end up with a black person. That is just one of the great tragedies of society. The last thing, incompatible personalities, is just a product of society. At some point, most couples just realize that they are too different and cannot be together. Nothing is wrong with this. In fact, this is what the whole process of dating is supposed to discover. Dating, the process of going out with people, is supposed to help someone find the person he/she is most comfortable with.

The way out

Everyone goes through life experiencing romantic relationships. But it is very rare that one of these relationships spans an entire lifetime. People have fun together but also, people often breakup. As one can see, there are many reasons why break-ups occur. These reasons can range from simply growing apart to finding your partner cheating or simply being too different to be together. These break-ups and reasons for them are not meant to scare someone away from relationships. The simple fact is, one should enjoy relationships, but at the same time, identify warning signs so one can see when a break-up is necessary.

Approximate Length: 1,031 words
Suggested reading time: 8 minutes
How fast do you read? _____

Comprehension Exercises

Complete the following exercises without referring back to the passage you have read.

1. The passage mainly deals with the negative consequences of break-up on individuals.
2. Everyone can find a perfect person once in a life time and live happily ever after.
3. Paying all the bills for your girlfriend may wear your love out and finally sets you two apart.
4. Gambling can be tolerated by one's partner sometimes.
5. A couple who go to the same college will get married.
6. When someone abuses his parents, it is time to have a break-up.
7. What we need to do is to enjoy the relationship and at the same time to keep an eye open.
8. When choosing new partners, one is often attracted to another person _____ his or her partner.
9. Finding your partner cheating will result in _____.
10. Differences in religion, different life goals, _____, and different family backgrounds could eventually lead to break-up.

Words & Expressions

1. **fallacy** *n.* 谬误；谬论
2. **abuse** *vt.* 辱骂；滥用
   e. g. abuse one's authority / sb. 's hospitability 滥用权威 / 辜负某人的热情招待
3. **break-up** 分手；离婚
4. **paralyze** *vt.* 使（某人）瘫痪或麻痹
   e. g. paralyze sb. with sth. 使某人不能正常活动
5. **incompatible** *adj.* 不相容的；不兼容的
   e. g. Their blood groups were incompatible. 他们的血型不相配。
6. **keep an eye open** 保持警醒
   e. g. While the mother is cooking, she keeps an eye open to the baby. 母亲一边做饭，一边关照着婴儿。

Notes

1. Whether it is an addiction to drugs, gambling, or whatever, hardly anyone would be willing to take that on an everyday basis. 不管是对毒品还是赌博的不良瘾癖，几乎没有人能够每天忍受它。
2. When someone abuses his girlfriend, spouse, or children, a break-up is definitely

necessary. 如果一个人虐待自己的女朋友、配偶或小孩的话，那就应该和他分手。

3. The simple fact is, one should enjoy relationships, but at the same time, identify warning signs so one can see when a break-up is necessary. 一个简单的事实是，我们应该享受恋爱和婚姻关系，但同时也应该能发现令人警醒的讯号，以确定是否需要分手。

 Key to the Exercises

1. N 2. N 3. Y 4. N 5. NG 6. NG 7. Y 8. besides
9. a lack of trust 10. different race, incompatible personalities

Passage 2

> **Directions**
>
> In this section, there is a passage with 10 blanks. You are required to select one word for each blank from a list of choices given in a word bank following the passage. Read the passage through carefully before making your choices. Each choice in the bank is identified by a letter. Please choose the corresponding letter for each item. You may not use any of the words in the bank more than once.

What Is an Ambassador?

What is an ambassador? Why do we need them? America maintains a diplomatic relationship with nearly 180 countries around the world. American embassies can be found from England to Micronesia to Brazil. An ambassador is the official ___1___ of the United States in each of these foreign countries.

An ambassador performs various tasks. They have many different ___2___. With the help of Foreign Service staff, they use diplomacy to promote United States' interests. An ambassador must have ___3___ communications skills and be up-to-date on the latest political atmosphere in a host country. They ___4___ constant communication with the State Department and other Executive Branch Departments. Ambassadors are always ___5___ to help Americans traveling abroad with situations they encounter. They may help them find medical care, help them with legal matters, and, under certain circumstances, an ambassador is responsible for ___6___ Americans from foreign countries. Ambassadors work hard to keep

American citizens safe in the world. Their goals include preventing war, ___7___ democracy, and advancing human rights. They may become involved in trade ___8___ and fighting the war on terror. They may also participate in negotiating treaties and ___9___ between America and other countries. Ambassadors travel around the host country learning about its citizens, customs, and landscape. They ___10___ welcome important visitors from the United States and host receptions to introduce them to diplomats and important citizens in the country.

Approximate Length：219 words

A. maintain	B. negotiations	C. reluctantly
D. withdrawing	E. suggestions	F. excellent
G. representative	H. reject	I. agreements
J. profitable	K. warmly	L. gathering
M. available	N. responsibilities	O. promoting

1. _____   2. _____   3. _____   4. _____   5. _____

6. _____   7. _____   8. _____   9. _____   10. _____

Words & Expressions

1. **ambassador** *n.* 大使

   embassy *n.* 大使馆全体官员；大使馆

2. **treaty** *n.* （国家或政府间的）条约；双人协议

   e. g. peace treaty 和平条约

3. **representative** *n.* 代表，代理

4. **negotiation** *n.* 谈判，洽谈

   e. g. be open to negotiation 可以协商

   　　　The terms of the contract are still open to negotiation. 合同条款仍可协商。

5. **landscape** *n.* （陆地上的）风景，景色；风景画

   e. g. the beauty of the New England in autumn 新英格兰秋色之美

6. **diplomat** *n.* 外交官；有手腕的人

Notes

1. America maintains a diplomatic relationship with nearly 180 countries around the world. 美国跟世界上大约180个国家保持外交关系。

2. An ambassador must have excellent communications skills and be up-to-date on the latest political atmosphere in a host country. 一个大使必须有卓越的交流技巧，并且掌握最新的政治动向。

3. Their goals include preventing war, promoting democracy, and advancing human rights.

4. 他们的目标包括:制止战争,促进民主,提升人权。
4. Ambassadors travel around the host country learning about its citizens, customs, and landscape. 大使们游历他们所待的国家,了解这个国家的人民、风俗和地貌。

Key to the Exercises

1. G   2. N   3. F   4. A   5. M   6. D   7. O   8. B   9. I   10. K

Passage 3

Directions

The passage is followed by some questions or unfinished statements. For each of them there are four choices marked A, B, C and D. You should decide on the best choice after reading.

The Experiences of Fear

Everyone experiences fear during major crisis, such as fires, automobile accidents, etc. Some people even feel very nervous when they fly in airplanes. No matter how hard they try, they cannot lower their anxiety. Some of them enjoy talking about their fears while others resent being asked to discuss their personal feelings. Many are aware that they feel anxious but only a few are conscious of the way they express their tension. Some people try to hide their nervousness: they try to disguise their anxiety by telling jokes. Others become loud and aggressive, attacking people by making them the butt of cruel jokes. Sometimes making someone else the target of jokes is an attempt to control one's own fears to master anxiety.

A number of factors can be mentioned as important in explaining why some people have a fear of flying: early childhood experiences, general sense of security, fear of heights, trust in other, percentage of alcohol in blood, etc. The memory of a bad experience can sometimes trigger the same fear caused by that experience. Thus, a child might be frightened by the sight of a dog even though he is safe, merely because he once had a bad experience with a dog. A bad experience can be the cue that triggers our fears. But the crucial factor seems to be a feeling of control.

Usually we are able to suppress our feelings so that they do not affect our behavior. But sometimes the tension produced by our fears is so great that we cannot suppress it. At such time we need to discharge the tension by laughing or crying. By smiling foolishly and talking loudly，we are able to repress（压制）the rising feeling of fear so that it does not affect the way we behave.

Because it is necessary to recognize a problem before it can be solved，admitting that we are afraid is an integral part of the process of mastering our fears.

Approximate Length：329 words

1. To make someone the target of jokes means _____ .
   A. to force someone to enjoy the jokes
   B. to entitle someone to tell jokes
   C. to offend someone by jokes
   D. to make someone become the object of jokes

2. What is the positive purpose of people's telling jokes?
   A. To disguise their anxiety.
   B. To attack others.
   C. To control one's own fears.
   D. To show one's sense of humor.

3. To master anxiety means _____ .
   A. to conquer the feeling of nervousness
   B. to hold back the feeling of uneasiness
   C. to be familiar with tension
   D. to be good at the subject of anxiety

4. According to the author，which of the following is the most important factor triggering the feeling of fear?
   A. Early childhood experiences.
   B. The general sense of security.
   C. The fear of heights.
   D. A feeling of no control.

5. According to the concluding paragraph，what is essential to go through the process of mastering one's fears?
   A. To be conscious of the way of mastering fears.
   B. To admit the feeling of fears.
   C. To control one's feelings.
   D. To repress the rising feeling of fear.

Words & Expressions

1. **resent** *vt.* 愤慨；怨恨
   e. g. resent sb.'s behavior 不满于某人的行为

2. **trigger** *vt.* 触发；引起
   e. g. The song triggered many happy memories. 那首歌勾起许多幸福的回忆。

3. **crucial** *adj.* 至关重要的
   e. g. crucial decisions 极重要的决定

4. **repress** *vt.* 压制；抑制；约束
   e. g. I could hardly repress my laughter. 我禁不住笑起来。

Notes

1. Some of them enjoy talking about their fears while others resent being asked to discuss their personal feelings. 一些人喜欢和别人讨论他们的恐惧，而另一些人则讨厌被要求去谈自己的感受。

2. A number of factors can be mentioned as important in explaining why some people have a fear of flying：early childhood experiences, general sense of security, fear of heights, trust in other, percentage of alcohol in blood，etc. 有几点重要的因素可以解释人在坐飞机时为什么会产生恐惧：儿童时期的经历，普遍的安全感，恐高，信任别人以及血液当中酒精浓度过高等。

3. Usually we are able to suppress our feelings so that they do not affect our behavior. 通常我们能够抑制住自己的感受而不让它影响自己的行为。

4. Because it is necessary to recognize a problem before it can be solved, admitting that we are afraid is an integral part of the process of mastering our fears. 因为在问题解决之前认识问题是很有必要的，所以承认我们害怕是控制恐惧过程中必要的一个环节。

Key to the Exercises

1. D   2. C   3. A   4. D   5. B

Passage   4

> **Directions**
>
> The passage is followed by some questions or unfinished statements. For each of them there are four choices marked A，B，C and D. You should decide on the best choice after reading.

The Pure and Applied Scientists

As the horizons of science have expanded，two main groups of scientists have emerged. One is the pure scientist.

The pure or theoretical scientist does original research in order to understand the basic laws of nature that govern our world. The applied scientist adapts this knowledge to practical problems. Neither is more important than the other，however，for the two groups are very much related.

Sometimes the applied scientist finds the "problems" for the theoretical scientist to work on. Let's take a particular problem of the aircraft industry: heat-resistant metals. Many of the metals and alloys that perform satisfactorily in a car cannot be used in a jet-propelled plane. New alloys must be used, because the jet engine operates at a much higher temperature than an automobile engine. The turbine wheel in a turbo-jet must withstand temperatures as high as 1,600 degrees Fahrenheit, so, aircraft designers had to turn to the research metallurgist (冶金学者) for the development of metals and alloys that would do the job in jet-propelled planes.

Dividing scientists into two groups—pure and applied—is only one broad way of classifying them, however, when scientific knowledge was very limited, there was no need for men to specialize. Today, with the great body of scientific knowledge, scientists specialize in many different fields. Within each field, there is even farther division. And, with finer and finer divisions, the various sciences have become more and more interrelated until no one branch is entirely independent of the others. Many new specialties—geophysics and biochemistry, for example—have resulted from combining the knowledge of two or more sciences.

Approximate Length: 271 words

1. The statement "the horizons of science have expanded" (Line 1, Para. 1) means that
   _____.
   A. the horizon is enlarged by scientists
   B. scientists can observe further space
   C. scientists are making efforts to expand the outer space
   D. science has developed more fields

2. The applied scientist _____.
   A. does original research to understand the basic law
   B. applies the results of research to practical problems
   C. is not interested in practical problems
   D. provides the basic knowledge for the pure scientist

3. The example given in the third paragraph illustrates how _____.
   A. applied scientist directs the work of the pure scientist
   B. applied science suggests problems for the basic scientist
   C. pure scientist operates independently of applied scientist
   D. pure scientist plays a more important role than applied scientist

4. Finer and finer division in the field of science has led to _____.
   A. greater interdependence of all the various sciences
   B. the elimination of the need for specialists

C. greater independence of all the various sciences

D. the greater need for the applied scientists

5. We can learn from the passage that _____.

A. both pure scientists and applied scientists are not equally important

B. the aircraft designer stands for the pure scientist

C. geophysics and biochemistry are examples of new specialties

D. pure scientists are more important

Words & Expressions

1. **emerge** *vi.* 浮现,出现;显露,暴露

   emerge from 从……出现

   e. g. The sun emerged from behind the clouds. 太阳从云层后露了出来。

2. **alloy** *n.* 合金

3. **withstand** *vt.* 耐得住,经得起;挡住,顶住

   e. g. withstand the test of time 经得起时间的考验

4. **interrelated** *adj.* 相互关联的,相互影响的

   e. g. Unemployment and inflation are interrelated. 失业与通货膨胀是相互联系的。

5. **combine** *vt.* 结合;使混合

   combine sth. with sth. 组合;合并;化合

   e. g. The new software package combines power with maximum flexibility. 这种新的软件包既有强大的功能又有最大的灵活性。

Notes

1. As the horizons of science have expanded, two main groups of scientists have emerged. 随着科学范围的扩展,出现了两种类型的科学家。

2. The pure or theoretical scientist does original research in order to understand the basic laws of nature that govern our world. 纯理论科学家负责基础研究以便于了解掌控这个世界的大自然的基本法则。

3. Sometimes the applied scientist finds the "problems" for the theoretical scientist to work on. 有时应用科学家也会为理论科学家发现问题。

4. And, with finer and finer divisions, the various sciences have become more and more interrelated until no one branch is entirely independent of the others. 而且,随着越来越细的区分,不同的学科之间的联系越来越紧密,没有一个分支是可以独立存在的。

Key to the Exercises

1. D   2. B   3. B   4. A   5. C